the breakfast club

D1412866

Kate Costelloe

MO24559

Hodder
Children's
Books

A division of Hachette Children's Books

First published in Great Britain in 2011
by Hodder Children's Books

1

ISBN-13: 978 1 444 90285 3

Typeset in AGaramond by Avon DataSet Ltd,
Bidford on Avon, Warwickshire

Printed and bound in Great Britain by
CPI Bookmarque Ltd, Croydon, Surrey

The paper and board used in this paperback by Hodder Children's Books
are natural recyclable products made from wood grown in
sustainable forests. The manufacturing processes conform to the
environmental regulations of the country of origin.

Hodder Children's Books
a division of Hachette Children's Books
338 Euston Road, London NW1 3BH
An Hachette Livre UK Company

To Lily for ideas and helpful insights,
and for Supriya for her musical advice

Chapter One

'*Hats?*' I said. 'Lexie seriously wants us all to wear hats to Mario's?'

It was a cold wet Friday in spring. School had officially finished five minutes ago. The other kids were abandoning the premises so fast they practically left vapour trails. Nat, Ella and I were the only ones still huddled just inside the foyer. Tiny cold drops blew in, spattering our faces as we clustered around Ella reading a surprising text from our friend Lexie.

'Are you sure this is from Lexie?' I asked doubtfully. Unless she's at the ice rink (she's a budding figure skater), Lexie's usual uniform is a hoodie and skinny jeans.

Ella seemed flustered. 'It *is* her birthday, Billie. She wants to look, you know, *stylish*, but in a hippie chick kind of way.'

'Hippie chick? Lexie? I'd have said that sounds more like you.' I gave Ella one of my looks and had the pleasure of watching my blond, fair-skinned friend gradually turn bright pink. If Lexie is the dynamic sporty one, Ella is like the Breakfast Club's boho princess.

'OK, it might have been my idea originally,' she admitted sheepishly, 'but she's totally into it now.'

'Does Lexie even *own* a hat?' I spluttered. Like everyone in the Breakfast Club, Lexie made an effort for our Saturday morning get-togethers at Mario's, but she's always been more into fitness than looks. Not that she needed to worry – Lex was one of those girls who looks good without even trying. All that skating means she always looks poised and elegant, and her long chestnut brown hair is annoyingly glossy. If we didn't love Lexie to bits, we'd totally hate her!

'I *definitely* don't own a hat,' Nat said glumly. 'OK, a riding hat, but I'm guessing that's not the look you're after, Ella?'

Ella gave Nat's arm a friendly pat. 'I can lend you one, don't worry. I've got one with beads like little raindrops. You'll look gorgeous in it.'

'Ah, one of those incredible magic hats,' Nat said with a sigh.

Nat has only been at our school for a couple of terms. She is tall and curvy and extremely feminine with wavy brown hair. She used to be totally clueless about clothes, but with our encouragement (especially Ella, who insisted on dragging Nat round all her fave vintage stalls), she is gradually finding her own style. But despite all our best efforts, she still doesn't have a grain of confidence.

'Magic hat!' What are you like?' I asked her sternly. 'Breakfast Club Rule Number 51A. All members are strictly forbidden to run themselves down!'

Nat looked genuinely thrown. 'We don't have rules, do we?'

'All clubs have rules, Natalie, or it isn't a proper club,' I said, straight-faced. 'In fact we've decided to get badges, haven't we, Ella?'

'Really tasteful ones,' Ella said playing along, 'with tiny fried eggs and bacon rashers.'

I nodded solemnly. 'Plus I've been giving this a lot of thought and I think we should all swear an oath of allegiance.'

Nat had been looking increasingly alarmed, until I got to the oath bit. 'Ha ha, very funny,' she scowled. 'You two are evil, you know that?'

3

Ella burst out laughing. 'Aww, come on, girl!' She linked her arm through an indignant Nat's. 'You know we love you. Don't we, Billie?'

'Yeah, but you're such a sucker! We can't resist,' I told her. 'Oh-oh, look out. It's the Fun Police!'

One of our least favourite teachers, Mrs Gildersleeve, hurried past, giving us her usual withering glance. The concept of fun is a hard one for long-faced Mrs G, who seriously doesn't look like she's ever had any. She spends break in the staffroom, drinking stewed tea out of her thermos, marking books and tutting every time somebody cracks a joke. We watched her get into her scruffy old vintage mini Cooper and adjust her mirrors.

I pulled up the hood of my big parka, tucking in a few kinky strands of hair. 'I should REALLY go to work.' I hauled my school bag over my shoulder to show I meant it.

'I've REALLY got to get my hair cut,' sighed Ella.

'And I've REALLY got to go home,' Nat said with a sigh. 'My stepmum is having a big family party.'

We exchanged reluctant grins, dumped our bags back on the floor and carried on chatting. We'd been together all day; tomorrow we'd be meeting up with Lexie, the fourth member of the Breakfast Club, at our fave Notting Hill café. You'd think we'd run out of things to say but we never did.

We also had another more personal reason for lingering. And suddenly here he was, hurrying out into the foyer, switching on his mobile: Mr Berolli, our new drama teacher.

'Oh God, he's *sooo* beautiful,' whispered Ella.

'Ssh', hissed Nat. 'I want to hear what he's saying.'

We all had a major crush on Mr Berolli but Nat was, like, obsessed. She had actually started a Mr Berolli file.

He gave us a distracted smile as he strode past. 'Hi,' he said to his unknown caller. 'Yes, I'm on my way now.'

Our eyes followed him with total devotion, taking in every tiny detail: his dark hair so black it was almost blue, the loose threads on his ancient winter coat (Ella reckoned he'd probably bought it from a charity shop), his red knitted scarf flying out behind him.

'Goodbye, darling Josh,' Ella said softly.

We had wondered about his first name for weeks. The brass initials on his leather briefcase were JB, but as Ella pointed out, the case could have been another charity shop find like the coat. Nat disagreed. She thought it was a graduation present from his proud parents and she thought the 'J' stood for Jake, because romantic heroes are almost always called Jake. Ella said no way would his parents call him something so cheesy. 'He's a James,' she'd insisted. Then one day the head called out, 'Josh, have you got a minute?' and we all clutched at each other mouthing, 'OMG! Josh Berolli!' It was the perfect name for him.

'You should write a song about him, Billie,' said Nat now as we watched Josh Berolli unlocking his car, a lovingly polished old Volvo.

'Yeah, Billie! We could go round to his house and serenade him,' Ella suggested, giggling.

I'm making us sound like silly lovesick girls, but our collective crush on Josh Berolli made us so incredibly happy I can't tell you, and it never interfered in the slightest with our fancying guys our own age. Ella went on fancying geeky Eddie Jones. Nat was in and out of love with a different boy every week, and I had my own private crushes which I occasionally shared with the other girls in the Breakfast Club.

But our feelings for handsome, sensitive Mr Berolli were totally different from our other crushes because they were shared. Josh Berolli was *ours*, and we loved him with a pure and protective love, even Lexie – and she'd only met him once in Waterstones. We'd gone in with Ella who was mad keen to buy the latest book in that sexy vampire series she's into. While we were hunting for the teens section we literally stumbled over Josh Berolli sitting cross-legged on the floor of the bookshop, leafing through a picture book about polar bears.

He looked up and saw us all shyly standing there. 'Oh, hi,' he said. 'I'm trying to choose a book for my little nephew for his birthday.'

'What's his name?' Nat put her oar in so quickly you could see her mentally adding another entry to her Mr Berolli file.

'Freddy,' he said, smiling. 'He's going to be four.'

We politely introduced him to Lexie, but it was like she'd gone into some kind of trance. Seriously, she couldn't move or speak. We had to take her into Starbucks and buy her a mochaccino.

'*Now* do you get it?' we kept saying. 'Can you see why we love him so much?' And Lexie had whispered, 'OMG, yes, he's *perfect*!'

One afternoon when we were all at Ella's, we'd had a lengthy discussion about exactly what it was that made Josh Berolli so perfect in our eyes. Nat, being Nat, wrote down all our comments for her file. This is what she wrote:

He has the most beautiful kind eyes. (Lexie)

He's young so he still understands what being young is like. (Me)

He doesn't care about clothes, he is just naturally cool. (Ella)

He plays seriously excellent music in his car. (Me)

He really looks at people when they talk. (Lexie)

And he really listens, not like most grown-ups. (Nat)

He's funny! (Ella)

He respects us but he doesn't try to be one of us. (Me)

He genuinely cares about people in poor countries. (Nat)

Nat had written that last entry because Ella, Nat and I had seen pictures of Josh Berolli on the school board looking tanned and incredibly relaxed in cut-offs, surrounded by laughing kids in Sao Paolo where he had helped to set up a project to run free drama workshops for slum kids. I mean, *serious* swoon.

As we watched Mr Berolli's gleaming Volvo ease out into the traffic, Nat said loyally, 'You can see he's an *excellent* driver.'

8

She and Ella both had identical wistful expressions. I knew how they felt. As Josh Berolli's car disappeared from view I felt as if a tiny piece of me had gone with him.

Nat hunched gloomily into her coat. 'My sisters are giving me a makeover before the party,' she told us.

Nat rarely talks about her real mum who died when she was still very small. I once made the mistake of asking if she still dreamed about her (I still dream about my dad all the time) and it was like she instantly put up this protective wall. 'Of *course* not,' she snapped. 'I was still in nappies when she died. I hardly even knew her.' Now it's almost like Nat's got three mums. Her older sisters, Nellie and Plum, and her stepmum are total control freaks, constantly trying to run her life. This includes random 'makeovers.' I don't know why Nat puts up with it.

I made a rude noise. 'Tell them thanks for the offer, but you can't improve on perfection.'

Nat gave a shriek of nervous laughter. 'I can just imagine their faces if I said that!'

'So say it!' said Ella. 'Seriously, Nat, you shouldn't let them boss you around. It's not like they've even got any *taste*!'

We had a collective shudder as we remembered Nat's

9

last 'makeover', achieved with a tight baby-blue body-con dress and red-hot straightening irons.

Nat's got gorgeous hair, an angelic heart-shaped face and peachy skin. In any language this equals 'drop-dead beautiful' – or so you'd think. But because she's also five foot eight and has (gasp!) *curves*, Nat's step-mum and sisters are constantly giving her a hard time.

I should explain that Nellie, Plum and Jenny (Nat's step-mum) are all spindly size-six stick insects who are also in a permanent strop because they're totally undernourished. When Nat first arrived at our school, her step-mum was forcing her to bring cottage cheese and rice cakes for lunch 'to keep her weight in check'. We soon put a stop to that.

'It's time someone explained to you that rice cakes are basically polystyrene sold under a different brand name?' I'd told Nat with a grin, and I'd dumped them in the bin. 'I'm sorry, Natalie, but eating polystyrene is just *wrong*.'

'Diets are for losers,' Ella had agreed. 'And you're not a loser, Nat.'

Nat had looked as if she was going to burst into tears. 'That's not what Plum and Nellie say.'

Believe it or not, those really are Natalie's sisters' actual names. Nellie was officially christened Eleanor, but she called herself Nellie when she first learned to talk so that's what everyone in her family still calls her. Nat's nickname is the worst. Her family call her 'Natkins', after Squirrel Nutkin in the Beatrix Potter stories. Plum isn't a nickname apparently; it's an old family name. Kind of makes me grateful I don't come from an old family.

We'd told Nat to forget Plum and Nellie. 'If you want a role model, we'll introduce you to Lexie. She's the healthiest, most energetic girl you'll ever meet,' Ella had said fiercely. 'And you don't see Lexie eating polystyrene, do you, Billie?'

I'd shaken my head. 'Curvy and happy, that's the way forward!' I'd temptingly held out a bag of yum-yums which Ella and I were sharing.

'Curvy and happy?' Nat had looked at the twisty little doughnuts as if they'd come hot and steaming from the Devil's own bakery. 'You don't really mean that.'

'Oh, yes we do!' we'd chorused like characters in a panto.

Nat had glanced round furtively as if Plum and Nellie might actually have followed her to school. Then she'd reached out, daringly broken off a piece of doughnut and popped it into her mouth to enthusiastic applause from her new mates.

Since then we have worked hard to persuade Nat that the world won't end just because she has an occasional helping of mash or pasta; and it's actually paying off. In fact, Nat is showing distinct signs of turning into a bit of a foodie – and of course Lexie, Ella and I make it our personal business to encourage her.

I finally hoisted up my bag, for real this time. 'I'll see you guys tomorrow at Mario's. I'll be a bit late,' I remembered. 'I'm dog-walking again first thing.'

'We'll have a latte waiting,' Ella promised. 'And a huge pile of raisin toast to keep your strength up while you read the menu!'

'And we're definitely wearing hats?' I asked, to double-check.

Ella nodded, beaming. 'You should wear your slouchy beanie, Billie. It makes you look like an off-duty celeb!'

'Billie always looks like an off-duty celeb,' Nat said wistfully.

I looked down at my school uniform in surprise. 'I don't think so!'

'You do,' Nat insisted. 'But I was more meaning outside school. You do that urban cool denim thing and on you it looks sooo good!'

'Hey! What about me?' With her perfect cheekbones and silky blond hair, Ella really doesn't need to fret about her looks, but like all beauties she enjoys being reassured.

'You're just a celeb twenty-four seven,' Nat said, laughing. 'People probably think you and Billie have hired me as your homely personal assistant.'

'Enough of the homely,' I told her. 'I'd kill for your curves, Natalie.'

Typical Nat didn't even register the compliment. 'You'd better get going fast, Billie,' she teased, 'before the paparazzi get on your trail!'

'I'd better get going or I'll be in big trouble with Mr Kaminski, more like,' I said, spotting the time. I gave them both quick hugs. 'Laters, OK?' Ducking out into the rain I hit the playground running.

In addition to my regular Friday evening job at Ozzie's collecting up glasses until nine o'clock, I'd acquired a new job, walking our neighbour's dog when I got back from school. I'd been walking Bullet ever since Mr Kaminski came out of the hospital following a bad fall. Like his owner, Bullet was getting old and slow. I just had to walk him round the block, wait for him to do his business (*euw*), then take him back home and collect my dosh.

The first time I'd done it, Mr Kaminski just casually mentioned that Bullet wasn't fond of police cars. Police cars are a fact of life around the Grove, where I live, but having met portly little Bullet I couldn't see a problem so long as I kept him on his lead. So far he'd been as good as gold, puffing along beside me on his stumpy little legs, sitting obediently at the curb when I said, 'Sit,' and following me across the street when I said, 'Over.'

This particular afternoon Bullet plodded patiently through puddles, occasionally stopping to snuffle at a lamp post. I was humming to myself, a little tune that I'd been working on for a while. Then the police car came screaming out of nowhere, blue lights flashing.

Bullet ripped his lead out of my hand and legged it in the opposite direction faster than you could say GONE. One minute he was there, the next he was this disappearing little dot!

I found him about a mile down the road outside a tattoo parlour, trailing his lead through a puddle and looking embarrassed. As I marched him back home I was already picturing my friends' reactions next morning as I told them my Bullet story. I imagined them all having hysterics as I told them, 'Now I know why he's called Bullet!'

This is why we all loved the Breakfast Club. No matter how rubbish our weeks had been, we knew that come Saturday, we'd be sitting in our special booth, breathing in Mario's signature scent (a mix of ground coffee beans, Italian chocolate, hot sugar and cinnamon), all talking at once, and suddenly all our troubles would kind of magically melt away.

We were all friends before we became the Breakfast Club, but post Breakfast Club the four of us have been, like, *totally* solid.

I'm so lucky, I thought. *I can't believe how lucky I am.* I was suddenly so ridiculously happy that I actually crouched down right there on the wet pavement to pat a surprised little Bullet.

When I let myself back into Mr Kaminski's house, he was snoozing in front of CBeebies and didn't actually notice that I'd kept his dog out thirty minutes longer than normal. Bullet dragged himself wheezing to his basket where he immediately fell into a stunned sleep. 'I won't tell anyone if you don't,' I told him as I tiptoed out.

I raced next door to our flat so I could change into the stupid little skirt and top I have to wear for my shift at Ozzie's. I quickly brushed my hair, tying it back off my face. My friends are always saying how they envy my thick, ringletty hair. I tell them it's OK for them; they don't have to constantly fight it with expensive products.

I gave a yearning glance around my cosy room. My life had been so hectic the past few weeks that almost the only time I got to be in it was when I was sleeping. Apart from my actual bed, almost everything in my room is music-related; posters, guitar, electric piano, decks (I'm what you'd call a bedroom DJ!). My room's not very big so I try to keep things tidy or it can get a bit insane.

I still had my little tune going round inside my head. My new song was at the stage where it was still just a tiny germ of an idea. It wasn't even an idea. It was actually more of a *feeling*. You know that feeling where it's like something major is missing and you feel this actual physical *ache* inside, but you don't really know what it is you're aching for? That was like the starting point for my song. I ran my fingers over the keys of my piano producing a few bluesy chords. 'Something's missing,' I sang softly. 'Something's missing but my friends all think I'm fine . . .' If I didn't have to go to Ozzie's, I could stay home and work on my song.

Any time I'm alone in my room, my eyes sooner or later go to my pin-board where I keep a curling photograph of me and my dad. I was three years old when it was taken. I've got enormous dark eyes, too big for my little pixie face, and a crazy cloud of Afro hair. In the pic, I'm sitting on Dad's knee while he shows me how to play an African drum called a *djembe*. Both of us are beaming at my mum as she takes the picture.

My mum told me that when my dad left, she cried herself to sleep for a week. Then she gave herself a stiff talking-to, signed up for night classes and got on with making a new life for herself and me. A few years later, she met Mitch, my step-dad (he's a social worker like Mum), and they had my little brother Finlay.

I'd love to be more like my mum, focusing on the future, but I don't seem to know how. Losing my dad created this huge scary gap in my world that I don't know how to fill. I act like it's not there, but I feel it every waking moment. First thing in the morning I open my eyes and I get this nightmarish sensation, like there's a huge hole in my world and I might fall in.

Ella thinks it's harder for me because Mum, Mitch and Finlay are all white, and I've got half my dad's Jamaican DNA. I disagree. I'm fine with Mitch, Mum

17

and Finlay being the way they are, like I'm also proud of looking how I look. My problem is that I am like my father's daughter on the *inside* too. Dad was a musician and so am I.

My step-dad *kind* of understands. OK, so music might not be Mitch's driving passion like it is with me, but in his own nerdy way it matters to him. He collects old vinyl from the golden days of Motown. 'Collection' sounds like it takes up a modest little shelf in our sitting room, but Mitch's collection outgrew its shelf years ago; these days it fills our entire box room! He also loves nerdy-type discussions like, which is the superior version of *The First Cut is the Deepest*? (I tell him it's the one by PP Arnold. No contest.)

My mum never ever talks about music, not if she can help it. She let me have piano lessons and she puts up with me endlessly practising, but she's always made it seem like music is some trivial noise people have on in the background while they're doing something more useful. But to musicians, like my dad and me, music isn't an optional extra. It's our life.

Mum hates it when I talk like this. She just about tolerates my hobby, but she's totally against it as a career. It's weird. In every other way you can think of, my mum is the most easygoing person you can imagine, but when it comes to music she has this complete blind spot. The last time I attempted to explain that I wanted to devote my life to writing songs and playing instruments, she literally slammed out of the house and didn't come back for over an hour.

You know what's really weird? I've never once heard my mum sing, not even in the bath. Even Mitch sings in the bath. Finlay sings in the bath (actually Finlay sings when he's on the toilet). Not my mum.

I know for a fact that my mum wasn't always so down on musicians. I once found an old photo of her in 1980s glad-rags in a crowded club, and her eyes are just shining with happiness.

I'm almost sure I know what made her change. A few weeks after the *djembe* picture was taken, my dad was offered a job playing in a club in New York. My mum begged him not to take it. One night, while she was giving me my bath, he packed his bags and left. I never even got to say goodbye. In fact I never had the chance to see or speak to him again ever. Not long after Dad went to live in the States, he died. It happened out of the blue. He came back from the club where he was working, sat down in his chair to relax after the show, and his heart stopped, just like that. When his flat mate came in a couple of hours later he thought my dad was just asleep. The doctors said it must have been like some kind of congenital weakness.

Now it's as if, because of what happened to my dad, my mum can't help connecting music with danger and heartbreak. But for me music is the oxygen I breathe, and if you can't breathe, you curl up and die, right?

I was still tracing my dad's smiling face with my fingers when I heard my mum's key rattling in the lock. I went into the hall and found her struggling in with the groceries.

When she saw me she dumped her bags on the floor and gave me a hug. 'Hello, stranger! You've usually left for Ozzie's by now.'

I started to tell her about Bullet and the police car, then realised my little brother was missing. 'Where's Finlay?'

'He's sleeping over at his friend Conor's. Mitch and I are having a night out.' She shot me one of her looks. 'Have you eaten anything since you got back? You haven't, have you?' How do mums *always* know? It's like they're psychic.

She watched sternly while I made myself a peanut butter sandwich. Still munching I ran to get my bus.

This is where my evening came unstuck. When the bus finally appeared, the driver must have seen me waiting, shivering in the rain, yet he went zooming past without stopping. It wasn't even full!

I should explain that I don't spend my Friday evenings racing around Notting Hill like a girl with her tail on fire just because I enjoy it. I do it so I can pay my share of the Breakfast Club's tab along with everyone else. If I didn't make it to Ozzie's in time to do my shift, I couldn't go to Mario's: it was that simple. Mum helps me out when she can but I'm fourteen now. I can't live off her and Mitch forever.

I decided I'd have to try to make it there on foot and hope Ozzie was in a forgiving mood.

I once won a medal at primary school for the short-distance sprint. Running all the way to Ozzie's was more like a marathon. I don't know if you've ever tried running a marathon in a tiny little skirt? I could feel stitches snapping all over. By the time I reached Portobello Market I was gasping like a fish.

Most of the stallholders had gone home while the rest were packing up, shunting rainwater off plastic awnings, throwing leftover stock into their vans. 'I thought the Olympics were in 2012!' one called. Everyone in Portobello thinks they're a comedian.

I hurtled on, swerving between stalls and around

puddles; then for absolutely no reason I slowed to a standstill and started hunting through my bag until I found my phone. Ozzie goes mad if he catches you using your mobile so I'd switched it off before I left. Now I switched it on again. I don't know why. When I told Ella later she said I must have picked up her stress vibes.

I'd got three new texts from the other girls in the Breakfast Club.

Even by our standards this was excessive. I'd only just said goodbye to Nat and Ella, plus I'd be seeing everybody at Mario's tomorrow. What had they got to text *about*? 'Must have decided against the hats,' I muttered, but really I knew that wasn't it. Then I read Ella's text. I read it three or maybe four times but I couldn't seem to take it in.

Nat and Lexie's texts basically said the same thing as Ella's. I refused to believe them. It couldn't be true.

I stood in the pouring rain, slowly absorbing Ella's shocking message.

Marios is closing

For the rest of the evening I was numb. I didn't even register Ozzie's scowls.

I should explain that quite apart from the Breakfast Club, I had a totally selfish and personal reason for wanting Mario's to stay open.

Mario's had a licensed bar where local musicians sometimes played live. A few days ago Mario's daughter, Jools, had told me she was planning a fundraiser for her friend Ann-Marie's little girl. Freya was three years old and she'd recently been diagnosed with autism. As if that wasn't tough enough, she'd been born with cerebral palsy. The doctors had told Freya's mum that Freya would probably never be able to walk, but she refused to believe it and started reading up on kids with cerebral palsy. While she was doing her research, she found out about a radical new treatment programme in Arizona that was getting spectacular results.

Jools had shot a movie clip of her friend's little girl on her phone. She showed it to me, then asked if I'd be willing to sing for free to help them raise the money to send Freya and her mum to Arizona. I'd said, 'Sure, why not?' Not letting on that it would be my first proper gig. Now the opportunity had gone POUF in my face and little Freya wouldn't be able to take part in the special treatment programme.

As I slotted endless dirty glasses into Ozzie's dishwasher, I made a mental list of all the reasons

Mario's couldn't be allowed to close.

Mario's made the best coffee in the entire Universe, so Ella said, and she's the Caffeine Queen. Their pastries were a local legend. They played music that my friends and I would have happily used for the soundtrack of our lives. Best of all, Mario's was *ours*; Ella's, Lexie's, Nat's and mine. We couldn't have found a better home for the Breakfast Club if we'd invented it ourselves.

After my shift was over I stood in Ozzie's doorway, sheltering from the rain, and called Ella. 'You actually know this for certain? Mario's is seriously closing?'

'Mario's isn't closing,' Ella said. I was about to wilt with relief when she added shakily, 'It's already closed.'

'*What?*'

Ella sounded like she was crying, 'They told me in the hairdressers, but I didn't believe them. I thought Jools would have said something, at least to you. So on my way back I stopped by Mario's to see for myself. Billie, it was horrible. They'd put the shutters up. It was totally dead.'

'But – why would they – I mean, so *suddenly*?'

I heard her blowing her nose. 'The recession, I suppose? Dad says businesses are going bust everywhere.

Sorry, Billie, I'm too miserable to talk.' My phone suddenly went dead.

All night, I'd been comforting myself with the thought that we could still go tomorrow. We could have one last Breakfast Club get-together. We could celebrate Lexie's birthday, with or without hats, and say goodbye to Jools and all the lovely people at Mario's.

It had never occurred to me that Mario's was already gone forever.

Chapter Two

That night, I couldn't get to sleep. Every time I shut my eyes I could see my hands slotting dirty glasses into Ozzie's space-age dishwasher, glass after glass after glass, and I'd hear Ella saying, 'It's not closing, it's closed.'

Around 4 a.m. I dropped into one of those black sleeps that leaves you feeling worse than if you'd been up partying all night. Then I heard running feet and a shouty little voice, followed by the sound of my door bursting open. Like all little kids, Finlay is ruthless. Too late, I pulled my duvet over my head.

'I know you're not asleep because your eyes were open!' he said accusingly.

'Because you woke me up, you little monster!' I told him, laughing.

I can never stay mad with Finlay for long. Some kids

have problems with their step-siblings, but my little brother and I had a special bond from the start. In some weird way, it's like I've always known him. I patted my bed and he landed beside me with a bounce. 'So did you have fun at Conor's?'

He shrugged. 'Meh.'

'Meh?'

'Conor's *boring*,' my brother complained. 'He goes on and on about bottoms. He actually thinks he's being funny.'

'I seem to remember you had a thing about bottoms once upon a time.' I tried to smother a yawn.

'I probably had a thing about them when I was *five*,' Finlay said with dignity. 'I'm five and a quarter now.' He jumped off my bed, flashing a missing milk tooth. 'Dad said to tell you he's making pancakes. Do you want some?'

'It's the Breakfast Club today,' I said out of habit, then it hit me all over again.

Mario's had been at the centre of our lives for six months. I couldn't believe it had gone. I closed my eyes to hide my tears and heard Ella's voice say clearly, *Am I the only person in this room who thinks being fourteen sucks?*

'Are you OK?' Finlay sounded puzzled.

28

I opened my eyes and gave him a watery grin. 'Tell Mitch I'd love pancakes. I'll just grab a shower, OK?'

My little brother ran off yelling 'DADDY!!! BILLIE SAYS SHE'D LOVE SOME PANCAKES!'

I padded across the hall to the bathroom.

Am I the only person in this room who thinks being fourteen sucks? Ella repeated in my head. I could hear the exact tune that was playing in the background at the moment she said those words; the unforgettable moment that had welded four West London girls from different backgrounds into the group we had jokingly nicknamed the Breakfast Club.

It was a Saturday afternoon, almost exactly five months ago. We were about a month into the autumn term and we'd made a date to watch a movie at Lexie's. Lexie has been friends with me and Ella since we were at primary school – we all lived close by each other. Then Lex's parents found the perfect new house in Shepherd's Bush and moved her away. We were all worried that Lex would lose touch with us – even find new friends to replace us! But we're closer than ever.

Her parents had gone out to meet one of their suppliers. They run their own organic delivery business, delivering veggie boxes all around West

London. They started it up a couple of years ago, just as organic food was taking off. Back then, people had been willing to pay whatever it cost to buy food that was free from toxic chemicals. But since the recession, Lexie's mum and dad had come under more and more pressure as they tried to keep their business afloat; working long hours, even working at weekends.

On our movie afternoon, Lexie had been left in charge of her boisterous little brothers. She's got three: Liam who's nine and almost civilised, and seven-year-old twins Clem and Cameron, aka the Devil's Spawn.

The boys were downstairs supposedly playing a computer game, but as usual Clem and Cameron had started messing around. Liam was getting frustrated because they were spoiling his game. Lexie said to ignore them but it got so we couldn't actually hear the movie through the mayhem. Eventually we switched it off in disgust, not so much because of the noise but because it was a rubbish movie.

'What a rip off!' moaned Nat. 'The trailer made it look SO cool.'

'That's why trailers were invented, to make movies look cool,' I said.

Nat shook her head. 'Billie, that movie *was* the trailer, plus, like, an *hour* of pure padding. They could have saved some surprises for the actual movie.'

'That's life though, isn't it?' said Ella in a tight voice. 'Hours of padding without any new surprises.' She was by the window staring out over the rooftops.

The rest of us exchanged looks.

'Fight with her mum,' Lexie mouthed.

When Ella gets like this, we've learned to leave her until she's ready to come out of it, so we dipped into the giant bag of Haribo I'd brought along, chatting amongst ourselves. Of course, it wasn't long before Nat started talking about Josh Berolli. Sometimes, though she would hotly deny this, Nat just likes to hear herself saying his name. She was just wondering out loud if Mr Berolli had a middle name, and if so how we could find out, when Ella burst out, 'I wish there was somewhere we could go, somewhere we could all hang out together—'

The rest of this sentence was drowned by furious bellows from downstairs. 'You plank!' and 'Don't you DARE call me a plank. YOU'RE a plank!'

'Aren't we hanging out now?' asked Lexie.

'I meant somewhere fun,' said Ella.

'Thanks a lot, Ella,' said Lexie.

Downstairs someone savagely turned up the volume on the TV. A man was ranting about car insurance.

Lexie marched to the top of the stairs and yelled down in her scary big sister voice: 'Turn that down you little morons or I'll tell Kathy and Will to confiscate all your computer games.'

The ranting instantly faded to a low grumble.

'—somewhere that isn't home or school,' Ella went on, ignoring the interruption. 'Somewhere we can just be us without people bugging us all the time.'

'Like my stupid little brothers,' Lexie agreed with feeling.

'Or someone's Mum bursting in because we've all gone quiet and she thinks we're all taking drugs,' I remembered with a grin.

Nat covered her face. 'Don't!'

Lexie hooted. 'Who knew Toblerone was a banned substance!'

Ella wasn't laughing though, so Lexie, Nat and I stopped laughing too, one by one. Downstairs Lexie's brothers had gone temporarily quiet. For a moment the only sounds were the muttering TV and the swoosh of traffic.

That's when Ella came out with the statement that changed our lives.

'"Happiest days of your life" – ha! Am I the only person in this room who thinks being fourteen sucks?'

We looked at her, amazed. Ella was saying what we all secretly knew, but had somehow never dared say out loud. The consensus among grown-ups seemed to be that if you weren't having a riotous time every single minute of your teens, there was something seriously wrong with you.

Nat gave a forlorn nod. 'I agree. It sucks.'

Ella collapsed on to Lexie's bed beside me and Nat. 'All we do is wait, wait, wait,' she said bitterly.

'I *totally* know what you mean!' Relieved that Ella was talking to us again, Nat was babbling in sympathy. 'It's like we're trapped in a limbo dimension, just waiting to grow up. If we were, like, *twenty* or something, it'd be a different story. We'd all have these glamorous jobs, we'd be renting a flat in Kensington . . .'

'Getting up late on Saturday mornings because we've been out clubbing the night before,' Lexie chipped in. This is one of our fave fantasies (OK, next to the ones about beautiful Josh Berolli).

'Then we all go out for breakfast in some cool little café, where we accidentally find ourselves rubbing shoulders with celebs—' I started.

I heard Ella whisper, 'Oh. My. God!' She sat bolt upright as if someone had jabbed her with a pin. 'We don't have to wait,' she breathed. 'We don't have to wait until we're twenty. We can have it now!'

Lexie gave a snort. 'Yeah, right! Who'd give us glamorous jobs? We'd be lucky to get a paper round!'

'Not the jobs, silly!' Ella's eyes were shining as if she was having some sort of vision.

'We definitely couldn't afford the flat,' Nat said sadly.

Ella sighed and it was an impatient kind of sigh. We weren't getting it. 'I love you guys. You're my BFLs, best friends for life. You're just the best, OK?'

'Anyone else feel a "but" coming?' Lexie asked us.

'But,' said Ella on cue, 'all the things we do – watching DVDs, snacking on Haribo, talking about Mr Berolli – we're just killing time until life finally gets interesting for real.'

'What's wrong with that?' demanded Lexie.

'Everything,' said Ella. 'Suppose our life was actually a movie.'

'It would be a really boring movie,' said Nat with feeling.

'Exactly!' said Ella, 'because we never DO anything!'

'I do loads,' objected Lexie. 'I help my mum and dad out. I go to the ice rink and practise my routines. I go to school.'

'What about all that dead time in between school and the ice rink and helping your parents?' Ella said.

34

'I do get what you're trying to say, Ella.' Lexie sounded huffy. 'I just don't agree. We don't only watch DVDs. We chat. We play Xbox. Sometimes we do karaoke. Besides, what are we *supposed* to do? We're fourteen. We have to live with our parents. We're broke.'

'I'll tell you what we do.' Ella jumped to her feet. 'We *stop* waiting. We take *control*. We *change* the boring movie and do something NEW!'

We were all staring at her with our mouths open. I felt my heart start to beat faster.

Ella was pacing now. 'Imagine all four of us waking up in our separate homes on a grey nothingy London day like today. At first no one feels like getting up, then you remember. Oh my God! It's Saturday! You jump in the shower, throw on your most stylish Saturday clothes—'

'Why are we putting on our most stylish clothes?' Lexie interrupted.

'I was wondering that,' said Nat.

Ella beamed around the room. 'We're going out to breakfast!'

'We are?' said Nat, surprised.

'Yes! Maybe we can't hold down jobs or rent our own place, or stay out all night clubbing, but we can still go out to breakfast in a cool café! We're living in one of the best, most vibey parts of London! We should go out and be part of it!'

Lexie frowned. 'So we meet up, eat breakfast, then what?'

Ella shrugged. 'Enjoy the ambience or whatever, talk about stuff, like our problems, what's happened in the week, plan our futures.'

'Let's do it,' I blurted out. 'It's a brilliant idea.'

Ella went pink. 'Seriously?'

'Seriously,' I told her.

Nat looked thoughtful. 'It's got to be the right café though.'

'Totally,' I agreed.

'Somewhere they don't give you the evil eye if you linger over your skinny *latte*.' For the first time Lexie sounded interested.

'And they've got to serve great coffee!' This was Ella, the coffee diva.

It was still a grey nothingy London day but Lexie's room was suddenly zinging with excitement.

Nat started scrabbling in her bag for a pen. 'Someone should be writing this down. OK. No evil eye, great coffee. What else?'

'Friendly but chilled,' I said.

36

Ella's eyes sparkled. 'Somewhere you could just casually happen to find yourself passing the sugar to Lily Allen.'

'Not so trendy you need to bring your personal stylist,' objected Lexie.

'Not scary trendy,' Ella agreed. 'But it's got to have a young vibe. Not one of those greasy spoons where sad old pensioners hobble in to keep warm.'

'It's got to be affordable.' (That was me.)

'Plus some of the breakfast options should be healthy,' Lexie said with a grin, 'or Mum and Dad will disown me.' As you'd expect, Lexie's organic-veg business parents are big on healthy eating.

'Are we really going to do this?' I was suddenly doubtful. 'It won't be like that time Ella said we'd be extras for that music video they were shooting in Portobello and you all bottled it, and I was the only numpty who turned up?'

'It won't be like the music video,' Ella promised.

'We'll have to try out loads of cafés though.' Nat waved her list. 'Which cafes do we know that fit all or any of our requirements?' Every now and then Nat sounds as if she's recently escaped from a posh boarding school, which she actually has. This was one of those moments.

'You can tear up the list, Natalie,' I told her confidently. 'We already know the perfect café, just around the corner from Hillgate Place.'

Ella slowly shook her head. 'Not ringing any bells.'

'Coffee beans?' I reminded her. 'You tracked them down like a little truffle hound.'

She gasped. 'Oh my God! Mario's!'

It was actually the first time Nat and Lexie had met. It was a crisp September afternoon and Ella, Lexie and I had bumped into Nat outside Notting Hill tube. We'd wandered along together chatting, then Ella started sniffing the air. We followed her up a narrow side-street as Ella's sensitive nostrils tracked the glorious coffee bean smell to its source. By now the aroma of fresh coffee was all mixed up with rich Italian chocolate, cinnamon and vanilla.

A girl was outside the café cleaning the windows. She saw us hovering, not sure if we should go in, and gave us a friendly grin. 'You girls look hungry,' she said. 'My dad has just made a fresh tray of *dolce*. Come in and try them.'

She was only a few years older than us, wearing well-cut black trousers and a crisp white shirt. She wore about half a dozen silver earrings in each ear, and a couple more in her nose. She'd stuck a red pencil jauntily through her thick curly black hair so she wouldn't lose it. Her name was Jools, and she was a future supporter of the Breakfast Club, though obviously we didn't know that then. We trailed after her into the café like little lambs and pigged out on her dad's freshly-made *dolce*, which were like delicious puffs of air filled with vanilla cream. We had drunk our coffees, eaten our *dolce* and left, totally forgetting that Mario's existed; until now.

'*I* remember now,' Nat breathed. 'They had those AMAZING pastries!'

'And cosy little booths like an American diner,' Lexie added, 'and photos of all their regulars on all the walls.'

'Oh! My! God!' Ella clutched dramatically at her heart. 'They had a photo of Lily Allen! Mario's is *totally* our perfect café!'

'Oh, yeah, she was with Dizzee Rascal,' I remembered. 'Dizzee's not local though. They must have been working on an album together.'

Nat perched on the edge of Lexie's bed, consulting her list. We could see her mentally ticking boxes. 'Billie's right,' she said in an awed tone. 'Mario's has got it all. Oh, wait, do we know if they serve good breakfasts?'

'Let's go next Saturday and find out,' I suggested.

Suddenly we were all hugging each other and squealing.

That was five months ago and we hadn't missed a single Saturday. We never did get to pass the sugar to Lily Allen (though Lexie once saw a girl who used to be in *EastEnders* coming out of the toilets), but now that we'd transformed ourselves into the Breakfast Club, we almost felt like celebs ourselves. We were inside our own Notting Hill movie, just like Ella said.

One Saturday I caught our reflections in the mirror over the bar as we were leaving. We had walked into Mario's as four girls with our separate worries, but we were coming out like a *unit*: strong, confident, happy and glowing. If I didn't know us already, I'd have wanted to be our friend.

Had it just all been too easy? We never had to search for our perfect café. We'd just stumbled on it by pure accident. Was that why it couldn't last?

Five months of happiness, I thought as I walked into the shower, closing the sliding door. A tantalising glimpse of what our lives could be, *should* be.

It should have been more, I thought, bitterly. And I shut my eyes as the scalding water came thundering down.

Chapter Three

There's another way I'm just like my dad, according to my mum. He never stayed down for long either. After a long, hot shower and a stack of Mitch's pancakes with maple syrup, I felt almost like the normal upbeat Billie again.

I texted my friends hoping we'd still meet up, but Ella was the only one who texted back. She said she was having a pyjama day but I could stop by so long as I got us some Krispy Kreme doughnuts on the way over.

Ella and her mum live in a cute mews-type cottage tucked away down a trendy little street off Portobello. They moved there soon after the split from her dad.

'Excuse the mess, Billie,' Ella's mum said as she let me in. 'It's a constant battle keeping things tidy in such a cramped space.'

Most people would absolutely kill to have the

Swansons' house but Annie's always going on about how it's like a poky little doll's house compared with the palace where her ex now lives with his new partner, not to mention Ella's new half-sister. (Seriously, she can't be mentioned, Ella says, or Annie turns into a total witch.)

Ella's mum is extremely good-looking, for an older woman I mean. Like Ella, she's blond with great cheekbones. She'd look even better if she wasn't always acting so sorry for herself. Everything is always like a huge drama for Annie.

She caught at my arm to stop me going through into the kitchen. 'I'm so glad you've come over,' she said in a stage whisper. 'Ella's been *so* upset.'

'We're all upset about Mario's,' I said.

Annie did that tragedy queen thing with her eyes. 'Not like Ella. The Breakfast Club meant everything to her. I didn't want to go out and leave her but I'd already promised to meet a friend. Life hasn't been easy for either of us since—'

'Don't worry,' I said quickly before she could get started on her divorce. 'I could do with cheering up myself. We can keep each other company.'

Not for the first time I thought how lucky I was to have my mum. Ella's always saying she wishes her mum could be more like mine. After my dad left we were really hard-up for a long time, but I never once heard my mum say anything against my dad. The opposite, if anything. She's always told me how proud he was of me and how much he loved me. Ella's mum talks about Ella's dad as if he's an evil genius who deliberately set out to destroy their happiness.

I heard Ella call out, 'I bet you didn't bring the doughnuts!'

'I did, actually, your Royal Highness! I got three different kinds.' I followed her voice into the kitchen, glad to escape.

'I'm making us cappuccinos, is that OK?' Ella said dully.

'OK?' I said. 'I'd *kill* for a cappuccino. I've been awake all night.'

In the time it had taken me to get to Ella's, my friend had showered and dressed in a soft grey hoodie and brand-new boyfriend jeans. Not pyjamas, but not Ella's usual flamboyant boho style either. She looked pale and subdued as she counted spoonfuls of ground coffee into a gleaming new coffee machine.

The Swansons' house might be old-style cottagey on the outside but inside it's got every technical gizmo you can think of. Unlike me and Mum, Annie and Ella never had to live on baked-bean soup after Ella's dad moved out. (There truly is such a thing as baked-bean soup. It makes a tin of baked beans stretch miles and is much less disgusting than it sounds.)

Annie had already shrugged on her long charcoal-grey coat, but instead of rushing off to meet her friend she kept hovering in the kitchen doorway, fiddling with the Cath Kidston scarf Ella got her for her birthday, and asking me how I was and if my mum was still enjoying her job working with the disadvantaged kids at The Kids' Company.

'It must be years since I've seen Nina,' Annie said wistfully. 'All four of us should get together some time for a girly night out. Wouldn't that be fun?'

'Totally,' I agreed, secretly crossing my fingers. 'You should call her and make a date.'

'Oh well. I'd better go and leave you girlies to your private chat,' Annie sighed at last. 'My friend is going through a really messy divorce and needs a lot of support. Men, eh?' she added bitterly.

It's only since her divorce that Annie has been so spiky. She used to be kooky and fun – a lot like Ella in fact. Our mums were at University together. I have a vivid memory of Annie and Mum running with Ella and me through the autumn leaves in the park when we were about six. Annie had started dancing around like a little kid, picking up handfuls of red and gold leaves and making them rain down on me and Ella. It was hard to believe she was the same person, I thought, as she picked up her Blackberry and reluctantly went off to meet her equally unhappy friend. These days Annie seemed permanently disappointed with everything.

After the door finally closed behind her, you could still feel the jangly, complicated vibe she'd left behind. Ella and I avoided each other's eyes as Ella brought us our frothy cappuccinos and I broke open the box of Krispy Kremes. We sat at the kitchen table, dropping sugary crumbs. Then Ella got up and turned the radio on to our favourite local music station and I started to relax.

'I got a text from Jools on the way here,' I said. 'She's really sorry she couldn't warn us.'

'Why didn't she then?' Ella said at once. 'I thought you and she were supposed to be, like, really tight? I suppose to her we're just giggly little girls, not worth bothering about.'

I rushed to defend Jools. 'She didn't tell us because she didn't know. Her dad's been keeping everyone in the dark.' Jools had sounded so upset in her text I'd phoned her to make sure she was OK.

'Their landlord was having financial problems and needed to sell up,' I explained to Ella. 'He offered Mario the chance to buy. Mario didn't have the money. On the other hand he didn't want his family worrying themselves sick about losing their livelihood, so he went round all the banks trying to scrape up the cash. The landlord got tired of waiting and sold the café over their heads.'

Now that she actually knew the facts, Ella's expression softened. 'Poor Mario, and poor Jools. Who did the landlord sell it to?'

I shrugged. 'Some property developer.'

'I bet they're all gutted,' Ella said.

'Totally. It was a real family business and they were building it up into something really special. They were just starting to get known.'

'You mean for the music?' said Ella.

'It was such a nice mellow little venue, Ella.' *And I was going to play at my first proper gig*, I thought, but I didn't say this out loud. I'd just lost an opportunity. Jools and her family had lost everything.

'It's bad enough to lose your business,' said Ella. 'But when it's your home . . .'

For a moment neither of us said anything. The radio

was playing a song called *Baker Street* by Gerry Rafferty which in my opinion has one of the most beautiful heartbreaking sax solos ever composed.

I could see Ella tearing up. There was something on her mind, I thought, something more than just losing Mario's.

'I want to show you something,' she said abruptly. She disappeared up to her room, coming back with a small stiff silver carrier bag, its handles prettily tied together with a loop of pink raffia. 'Look inside,' she said glumly.

I peeped into the bag. I could just see lots of pink tissue.

'Unwrap it,' said Ella. She gave a nervous glance at the kitchen door as if she thought her mum might come bursting in. Whatever was in this bag, Ella didn't want Annie to know.

I brushed doughnut sugar off my hands and carefully unfolded the tissue. Inside was a pair of doll-sized Nike trainers in dazzling pristine white.

'OMG! How cute are these?' I breathed. 'Are they for Kitty?'

Kitty was Ella's little half-sister. Her full name was Kitty Saskia Honey. I'd never actually seen her but Ella had shown us pictures of a beaming little girl with a huge patch of dribble on her front and absolutely no hair.

Ella shot another involuntary glance at the door. 'I don't know if they'll fit her now. I bought them weeks ago.'

I didn't ask why Ella didn't just give the shoes to Kitty. I knew why. Ella's mum had been reasonably OK about her ex-husband's access visits until she found out Naomi was having a baby. Since then she'd pulled every trick in the book to keep Ella and her dad apart.

I saw Ella blink back tears. 'I don't know what to do, Billie,' she wailed. 'I don't want to upset my mum but I really love my dad. I miss him, you know?'

'Of course you miss him, he's your dad,' I said gently. I carefully folded the dinky little trainers back inside their tissue and popped them into the bag.

'And I know I probably shouldn't but I really *like* Naomi.'

Ella's dad worked for a major TV company. He'd first got to know Naomi when she was working as his personal assistant. From the pictures Ella had shown us I thought Naomi looked OK.

'She seems like fun,' I said. 'I don't think you should have to feel guilty about liking her.'

Ella looked confused. 'Don't you, honestly? I just

feel like it's so disloyal to my mum. But they're so good together, Billie. Naomi has made my dad lighten up loads. You know what a workaholic he used to be. And OK, so they shouldn't have had an affair, but things weren't that great between Mum and Dad even before he started seeing Naomi.'

I remembered Ella coming to school with dark circles under her eyes having spent the night listening to her parents fighting downstairs.

Ella carefully rethreaded the fancy raffia through the handles of the carrier bag. 'This is going to sound awful, but it was a major relief when Mum and Dad finally split. OK, I still wish it hadn't happened. Sometimes I feel so mad with him, you know? But mostly I'm just grateful they're not yelling at each other like before. And he's a brilliant dad, Billie. He knocked himself out trying to make it up to me after the divorce, taking me out by myself so I didn't always have to share him with Naomi, and Naomi never minded. She never seemed like she did anyway.'

It seemed like everyone had behaved really well after the divorce, except for Ella's mum.

'I thought she'd, you know, *adjust*,' Ella said miserably. 'I mean, if I can accept what's happened, why can't she? But it's like I'm constantly tiptoeing around her, you know? One minute she's acting normal, then someone mentions Dad or the new baby and – I'm not joking – she practically grows fangs. She just won't accept Dad leaving. I'm starting to worry that she never will.'

'Why don't you just post them to Kitty?' I suggested, nodding towards the carrier bag. 'I'll post them for you if you like.'

Ella brightened for a moment. 'Would you really?' Then her face fell. 'Wouldn't that be, like, incredibly unkind to Mum?'

'Ella, Kitty's your baby sister! Whether your mum likes it or not, she's a part of your life and you should be part of hers.'

'That's true,' said Ella, half to herself.

'I wish I'd had a big sister like you for back-up,' I told her, patting her hand.

Ella gave me a watery smile. 'Thanks, Billie. I didn't mean to just dump my worries all over you. I feel bad whingeing to you about not seeing my dad. At least I can still text him and stuff even if I don't get to see him all that often, but you'll never be able to see—'

'Oh, hey,' I interrupted quickly. Ella was just trying to be sensitive but I always get twitchy when people talk about my dad. 'I was just a little dot when he died.

50

He was never a major part of my life like your dad was part of yours.'

For a moment I saw myself in the bath, a skinny three-year-old with a dandelion fluff Afro, chatting innocently to my mum, never dreaming that my dad was creeping out of the front door with his bags. *Just a tiny little dot.* How could you do that to me, Dad? How could you leave without saying goodbye?

When Ella's door bell rings it sounds like a rather grand peal of bells.

Ella was instantly on her feet, ready to race upstairs with Kitty's trainers.

'Your mum wouldn't need to ring, she's got a key,' I pointed out.

I followed her out into the hall and Ella put her eye to the tiny peep-hole. 'Lexie!' she yelled and flung open the door.

Lexie must have come straight from the ice rink. She'd thrown her raincoat over her skating things and carried her ice skates slung awkwardly over one shoulder by their laces to leave both her hands free. She needed them to hold the giant cake box from The Hummingbird Bakery, one of our all-time favourite cake shops.

'Happy birthday to me!' she warbled. 'I was nowhere near your area,' she added with a grin, 'so I thought I'd drop in. I even wore a hat, look!' She gave us a twirl, showing off her cute Fairisle beret.

Ella and I were SO ashamed! Caught up in our worries about Mario's we had totally forgotten Lexie's birthday.

Typical Lexie, she just waved away our apologies. 'Don't worry about it. I was so freaked about Mario's *I* almost forgot my birthday too. I went down to the ice rink as soon as I got up. Skating generally clears my head, only this morning it didn't seem to be working. Then I thought, actually Lexie, you need to be with your friends.'

I wish Lexie's parents hadn't moved from Notting Hill to Shepherds Bush; then we could still see her every day. Lexie is such a special person, like a breath of salty sea air. Just being with her gives me an instant energy recharge.

She dumped her skates in the hall and shrugged off her coat. 'I expect Nat's here already?' she said, beaming.

I shook my head. 'We've been trying to get hold of her but she's not picking up. They had a family party, remember? It could have gone on really late.'

We followed Ella into the kitchen. Ella started finding clean cups and making a fresh pot of coffee. Lexie opened the cake box. 'Ta da!'

I was expecting one big birthday cake but the box was full of gorgeous little cupcakes. Like a pack of Love Hearts, each cake had a feel-good word or phrase iced on it in brightly coloured icing.

'Wow!' Ella and I said, impressed.

'Those must have cost a LOT,' I added.

'Will and Kathy paid,' Lexie grinned. She and her brothers always call their parents by their first names.

'Even though it's not made of organic carrots?' Ella teased.

'They felt sorry for us because of Mario's so they made an exception. Dive in!' she invited.

'You first, you're the birthday girl,' I told her.

Lexie helped herself to a cake that said SWEET THING. She studied her message for a moment then took a huge bite. 'So what's the plan?' she asked with her mouth full.

Ella looked bewildered. 'What plan?'

'For the Breakfast Club, you bird brain, what did you think?' Lexie said impatiently.

'There's nothing to plan,' said Ella, looking upset. 'Mario's *was* the Breakfast Club, they're both gone. End of.'

I shook my head. 'That's SO not true.'

'I agree with my sister Billie here!' Lexie knocked fists with me. 'Mario's was great but it wasn't the Breakfast Club. *We're* the Breakfast Club.'

'The Breakfast Club is way bigger than any one café, even Mario's,' I agreed. 'It's about *us*: you, me, Lexie and Nat. You showed us that, Ella. You told us we had to get off our bums and change the movie. You said we had to take control of our lives.'

'I did, didn't I?' she said almost to herself.

I lightly smacked her hand. 'Yes, you did, so you can't just let it all go without a fight.'

'So what are we going to do?' asked practical Lexie. 'How are we going to save the Breakfast Club?'

Ella was suddenly sitting up straight. 'I suppose,' she said slowly, 'that we have to start looking for a new café.' She gave a little gasp as a new idea took shape. 'It could be like a *quest*!'

Lexie gave me a grin. 'She's *back*!' she said in a movie-trailer voice.

'We had beginner's luck with Mario's,' Ella said. 'This time we'll probably have to try a few different cafés for size.'

'Like, *audition* them?' I suggested, laughing.

'Yeah, good word, Billie. We'll audition them,' Ella agreed.

'If they don't make the cut, they're out,' said Lexie.

Life is so strange, isn't it? Last night it was like our world had ended, but just saying out loud that we wanted the Breakfast Club to keep going instantly sent our energy soaring. We still had a future. We still had the power to change the movie.

Ella helped herself to a cupcake and showed us her iced message.

It said: SAY YES!

'*Yesss!*' we shouted with one voice.

'Try Nat's mobile again,' said Lexie.

'Yeah, tell her we're re-launching the Breakfast Club,' Ella added.

'Re-launching, I like that,' Lexie said, grinning.

I don't know how many times we tried Nat's number. We texted her, we left voice messages. Nothing. We even emailed her. Still nothing.

Nat is a chatty, sociable person. Like the rest of us in the Breakfast Club, she can talk on the phone for hours about absolutely nothing. The only time she ever drops off our radar, like now, is when she's hurt or upset. When Nat's feelings are hurt she's like a little snail shooting back into her shell for safety.

We tried to think how we could reach her. If it was anyone but Nat we'd have simply turned up on the doorstep with the box of cupcakes. However, Nat's home is not the kind where you just 'turn up'. Out of the four girls in the Breakfast Club, Nat is *way* the most posh. The Bonneville-St Johns are actually connected to royalty on her dad's side. They've got a town house in Kensington Square and a rambling manor house in Norfolk where Nat and her sisters keep ponies. I think Nat is the first person in her family who has even been inside a state school. That's because she was so desperately unhappy at her (very famous) girls' boarding school that her dad finally stepped in, totally against her step-mum's wishes, and took her away.

All through Saturday and Sunday, Nat remained worryingly silent. By Sunday night I started to think she might actually be ill. To distract myself I started mixing a CD for Lexie's birthday. I'm always mixing special CDs for my friends, mashing up golden oldies together with the latest hits and various atmospheric sounds: Finlay chatting, my friends laughing, the sound of rain or passing traffic, all mixed in with snatches of my own tunes.

My starting point for Lexie's birthday CD was The Skaters' Waltz. This is obviously not my kind of music or Lexie's. It was just, like, a jokey reference, and a background for me to chat over.

I had written a little poem about Lexie: how she was a super-cool ice queen when she was skating, but in real life she was like a ray of sunlight in the dark, always there when her friends need her. I mixed in one of our favourite hip hop tracks, fading it in and out of the waltz together with samples from songs that I knew Lexie really loved, plus a movie track I found online. It was written and sung by someone called Mari Boine. I can't understand one word of her lyrics because she's from the Arctic Circle (where they have the Northern Lights) but she has the most heartbreakingly beautiful voice I have ever heard.

I was really getting into my mixing when my mum came in with the phone. 'It's Nat,' she mouthed. 'She doesn't sound too good.'

I took the phone and my mum tactfully snuck back out. 'Where've you been, girl?' I demanded. 'We've been trying to get hold of you all weekend.'

I heard Nat swallow hard. 'You know you said not to let my sisters give me a makeover?'

'Nat, you *didn't*.'

Nat told me that after she saw the results of her sisters' 'improvements', she was such an emotional wreck she hadn't even thought to check her messages.

She had no idea we'd been trying to get hold of her. That meant she still thought the Breakfast Club was dead and finished.

'I know you all think I'm pathetic for being such a pushover,' she wailed, 'but you don't have to live with them, Billie! Nellie said I'd be letting them all down. They said someone had to take me in hand.'

I felt myself getting hot with rage for my friend. Nat didn't deserve this. No one did. 'What did they do to you this time, Nat? Did they make you wear the scary magic knickers?'

'I didn't mind the scary knickers so much,' said Nat miserably, 'it's what they did to my hair. Plum said straightening my hair last time had killed her straightening irons, so they slicked it back with this icky hair wax then they put, like, a ton of shimmery blue gunk on my eyes. Honestly, Billie, I looked like something out of Avatar!' I heard her do a snuffling little giggle. Nat can usually see the funny side even when she's upset.

Nat said when she saw the results of their makeover in the mirror she fled up to her room in tears and barricaded herself in.

(I don't know how this happened but Natalie had somehow landed the smallest, dingiest bedroom in the house. It's just along the corridor from the airing cupboard, so she has to listen to the hot-water tank gurgling all night long. Inside her room there's space for a single bed, a desk, a chair, a chest of drawers – and that's it. Nat has to hang her clothes in Nellie's wardrobe.)

Nat described how her step-mum, Nellie and Plum took it in turns to shout through her bedroom door, trying to shame her into coming downstairs. I don't know what her dad was doing while this was going on. Nat says if anything happens at home that looks as if it might involve raised voices, he suddenly remembers he's got an urgent business call.

'Nellie said . . . She said they were only thinking of me.' Nat's voice had developed a dangerous wobble. 'She said I'll never be able to get a boyfriend if I don't do something about my looks.'

I couldn't believe what I was hearing. Plum and Nellie have boyfriends who work in the city. They are called something like Jed and Ned (me and Ella call them Ben and Jerry). They wear blue striped shirts and bellow into their mobiles all the time like braying donkeys. 'Would you *want* a boyfriend like Ben or Jerry?' I asked her.

'*No!*' Nat choked, 'but Billie, they said I'm like a

baby *elephant*. They said no one will EVER fancy me looking like I do.' And she burst into tears.

'Nat, listen to me,' I said urgently. 'They are talking out of their rear ends. Boys will SO fancy you, Natty, I swear. One of these days you will be beating them off with a stick.'

'Not really hot guys like Mr Berolli!' she wailed. 'My life was rubbish before we started the Breakfast Club, Billie. Now it's going to be rubbish forever.' She was sobbing now, big tearing sobs.

I knew she was too upset to take it in, but I had to try and tell her the good news.

'Nat! Stop crying and listen to me!' I raised my voice to make myself heard through Nat's hysterical tears.

I could hear Nat trying hard to pull herself together. She blew her nose and took several shuddering gulping breaths. She let out one more desolate little wail but I could tell she was getting there.

'That's better, you're doing great,' I said, sounding like a paramedic. 'Now have you still got puppies in your house?' Nat's step-mum breeds and shows cocker spaniels.

Nat gave a guilty little giggle. 'Betty's on my bed now. I smuggled her up inside my dressing gown.'

Betty is short for Ugly Betty. She's not ugly at all;

she's as cute as a button. She's just very small, the runt of the litter born several hours after the others – and so not suitable for enrolling at the Kennel Club or Crufts or whatever.

I pictured the Bonneville-St Johns' enormous rambling old house: the floors covered with antique rugs that have been nibbled and peed on by countless baby spaniels, the walls crowded with gilt-framed paintings of Nat's long-faced, pointy-nosed ancestors. And all alone at the top of that huge house, wrapped in a shabby old dressing gown and crying her eyes out, was Natalie Cordelia Bonneville-St John.

I would cry if my parents had called me Cordelia and I would throw a major tantrum if I had to wear Nat's hideous dressing gown. If you ask me, it should have been torn up to line Betty's basket. Like their Persian rugs, it was so faded and threadbare you totally couldn't tell what colour it was meant to be.

My mum once explained to me that Nat's family were 'old money'. According to Mum, people who are 'old money' are so sure of their place in the world that they don't feel the need to show off by buying anything new and shiny. They leave the showing off to 'new money'.

'Then Nat must have been swapped at birth,' I'd

told my mum. Natalie is SO not sure of her place in the world. She has, like, *zero* self esteem. I actually think we got to her just in time, before she faded away altogether.

'Are you cuddling the puppy?' I asked a still sniffling Nat. 'I'm not telling you my news until I know you're cuddling Betty.'

'Just picking her up now,' she gulped. 'Oops . . . I'd better mop up, hang on.'

I pictured Nat in her dog-blanket dressing gown mopping up after a gorgeous little floppy-eared puppy. That felt better.

'I'm cuddling her now,' Nat reported at last. Her voice gave another wobble. 'Is it very bad news then?'

'No, it's actually extremely good news,' I said firmly. 'Listen to me, girl. The Breakfast Club is *not* over. Ella, me and Lexie have had a talk and we're not giving it up, OK? We've just got to find a suitable venue.'

To my dismay Nat let out another wail. 'Suitable! Who wants *suitable*? We had *perfect*. You know it's true, Billie so don't say it isn't.'

'Nat, sometimes you just have to move on. You know what my step-dad said? He said, there's no reason the Breakfast Club should be limited to one place. He said it should be "a movable feast".'

There was a pause, then I heard Nat take a breath. 'A movable feast,' she repeated in a teary voice. 'I like that.'

I liked it too. Mitch said he borrowed it from someone called Ernest Hemingway.

'So that's all we're doing, Nat, OK? We're just moving the feast to another part of Notting Hill. So tonight, before you go to sleep, try to have a think about fun new cafés.'

Nat was blowing her nose. I could feel her trying to take in what I'd told her. 'There's Books 'n' Bagels?' she said tentatively.

I didn't want to knock her back after she'd been so upset so I didn't tell her that Books 'n' Bagels was probably only fun if you had an OAP bus pass. I just said brightly, 'Thanks, Nat! I'll tell Ella to put it on our list.'

'Hey, I know!' she said in a totally new tone of voice. 'Why not ask Mr Berolli? I bet he knows plenty of cool places to go!'

I was smirking as I put down the phone. If Nat was back to thinking about Mr Berolli she was definitely on the mend. My work was done.

Chapter Four

The alarm on my mobile always starts very softly; then, if I don't reach it in time, it quickly gets louder and crazier, adding clanging bells and piercing whistles until it reaches a huge mad crescendo. Next morning, I slept right through the intro. I slept through the whole shebang until my entire room was literally pulsating like some kind of hell disco.

I shot upright, gasping – and there it was again, that nightmare feeling. I don't know if this is something that happens to other people. It's not something you can really ask. It's been happening to me since I was four years old and my mum had to tell me that my dad was never coming home.

It feels like, every night while I'm sleeping, this, like, terrifying crater opens up in my world and I have to spend the first minutes of my day tiptoeing very gingerly around the edges, trying not to fall in. Nothing in my world feels safe or solid, least of all me.

I don't actually *think* about missing my dad, not in so many words. Everything just feels dangerous and *really* empty. It's like, when he died, he left this massive space that nothing and no one but my dad can ever fill.

Once I'm up and getting on with stuff, the feeling doesn't exactly go away; it's more that it gets camouflaged under everyday life. I'm able to act nearly like a normal person, a person who hasn't got an imaginary hole in the centre of her life. Sometimes I almost don't remember it's there.

By the time I had showered, dressed and walked Bullet once round the block I pretty much had things under control. I took Bullet back home, helped Mr Kaminski get his arms into his jacket sleeves (he'd got into a bit of a muddle), flew back home, grabbed my books and rushed off to school.

I walked through the gates at the exact same moment as the Alpha Girls.

Believe it or not, this is the name they picked for themselves. They see themselves as, like, the natural leaders of the pack, which I guess makes the rest of us pond life or whatever? 'Hiya,' I said cheerfully.

The Alphas flashed me their cool meaningless smiles, then immediately turned away. *Yep, definitely pond life*, I thought, grinning.

In order of Alpha-ness, the Alphas' names are Pia, Danni and Isabella. There's also Tamsin, who is like a wannabe Alpha. Tamsin always makes me think of a squirrel, I don't know why. It's not just her sandy colouring, or even that she's petite; it's how she watches people with darting green eyes, like she's secretly weighing up what they've got that she hasn't.

Tamsin very nearly made it into the Alpha's magic circle but failed to qualify at the last minute. Sadly, it hasn't dawned on her that this decision is final, so she hangs about hungrily on the outer edges, waiting to be invited in out of the cold. Now and then the Alphas decide to include her, but only for the pleasure of shutting her out later. Nat says it's a power thing. She said girls played poisonous power games like that all the time at her boarding school. This is one reason Nat gives the Alphas such a wide berth.

Like most London schools, ours is extremely international and so are the Alphas. Isabella's French. She's really pretty but incredibly spoilt. Danni is half-Chinese, clever, super-cool, *deeply* scary. Pia is Russian. The rumour is that her dad used to own half of London

67

and was basically like a billionaire or something. Then he lost most of his money on some dodgy property deals, and that's why Pia has to slum it at a state school. Pia compensates with her imperious attitude – she can pout for Notting Hill, and she has cheekbones to die for.

We have never gone out of our way to appease the Alpha Girls, yet miraculously we've never yet made it on to their (extensive) hate list. Nat says we're like those little animals in safari parks that are tolerated by bigger more powerful animals just so long as the water hole doesn't totally run dry.

If our class was a safari park though, Angelina would *definitely* be prey. Not because she's poor: Angelina's parents are seriously wealthy. They adopted Angelina when they were living in Nigeria. Her dad was out there working for some big oil company. Angelina is tiny, beautiful – and *really* smart. The only reason the Alpha Girls can find to despise her is that she's ill.

Last year, after endless tests, Angelina was diagnosed with Crohns disease. Crohns is a disease of the intestines that leaves you in constant pain. Angelina didn't want to tell us at first, she said she was too embarrassed. I told her, 'Why, girl? It's not like you're doing it on purpose!' Having Crohns makes Angelina incredibly tired, plus, because she can't actually absorb her food, so she isn't growing properly.

I'm not sure why being leaders of the pack means you mustn't ever show sympathy but that's the Alpha Girls for you. They actually make out that Angelina's faking her symptoms so she can have time off school. Unbelievable, I know.

This particular morning, barely half an hour after school started, Angelina suddenly doubled over in agony and Nat had to take her to the school nurse. Sometimes the nurse just lets her rest and then she rejoins our class, but if it's a really bad bout, the school phones home and someone waits with Angelina until their housekeeper comes to collect her. This was a bad bout. When Nat eventually came back I could see she was upset.

'Is Angelina OK?' I mouthed.

Nat just shook her head at me and mouthed back, 'Tell you later.'

At lunch time Nat mysteriously vanished, leaving me and Ella to grab our favourite table. 'I've drawn up a list of possible cafés,' Ella began but I shook my head.

'We should wait for Natty.'

'I feel like I'm doing a lot of waiting for that girl just lately,' Ella grumbled.

By the time Nat showed up, Ella and I were brushing our crumbs back into our lunch boxes.

'You look terrible,' Ella told her bluntly.

'I feel terrible.' Nat collapsed into a chair. Her face was chalky pale like she'd had some kind of shock. Her hair also seemed less bouncy and curly than usual. That was probably down to too much gel and mousse applied by her sisters.

'What happened?' I asked anxiously. 'Did they have to rush Angelina to hospital?'

She shook her head. 'It's not Angelina, it's Mr Berolli.'

Ella gasped. 'They rushed *Mr Berolli* to hospital?'

'No, of course not!' Nat said, horrified.

'*What* then?' Ella and I said simultaneously.

Nat felt unable to tell her story until she'd had some reviving swigs from her juice box. 'When I tell you, you're going to be SO upset,' she warned.

'OK,' we chorused nervously.

Nat set down her juice. She started tugging at one of her dark curls, a typical Nat distress sign. I saw her take a big breath. 'After I took Angelina to the nurse, I saw Mr Berolli's Volvo come scorching into the car park.'

Ella giggled. 'Dramatic! He must have overslept.'

Nat shook her head. You could see that she could hardly bring herself to say the words. 'He wasn't alone. Miss Simpson was in the passenger seat.'

'OK,' said Ella. 'And?'

'You don't get it, Ella. I skulked about a bit because I wanted to know what was going on, so I saw them coming into school together and they were, like, all giggly because they were late and they were being REALLY friendly.'

'Mr Berolli and Miss Simpson? You mean, like, an *item*?' I gasped. 'Are you sure you didn't inhale something funny in the medical room?'

She shook her head. 'It's totally true. Sick but true.'

'NO way!' Ella said. 'Not Miss Simpson – she's got to be at least thirty-five!'

'Ella, I swear! She was standing like bare inches away from him and she touched his arm – and she called him Josh. I can tell you her exact words. She said—' Nat's lip trembled and she had to start again. 'She said, "Thank you SO much, Josh, you are my hero!"'

'She *didn't*.' I was horrified.

Ella shuddered with disgust. 'I'm sorry but that is just *wrong*. I mean, Josh Berolli getting it on with Miss Simpson? Miss SIMPSON of all people!'

People were turning to look. Ella was almost shouting in her distress.

'*Sssh*,' said Nat. She lowered her voice. 'I couldn't believe it either, so I thought up an excuse to go into the staffroom just now and he was *sharing her quiche*!'

'He could have just forgotten to bring lunch,' I suggested.

'How did you get into the staff room?' Ella asked with interest.

'I said I thought I'd seen someone try to steal Mrs Gildersleeve's car.'

I let out a hoot of laughter. 'You didn't!'

'I was on a mission,' Nat said defensively. 'I needed to see for myself.' Her face crumpled. 'Now I wish I hadn't.'

'*We* should bring lunch for Mr Berolli one time,' Ella suggested.

'We could make up a little picnic to share,' I agreed. 'Just something very simple: smoked salmon, caviar, quails' eggs, chocolate mousse . . .'

Even Nat managed to raise a grin. 'That'll teach Miss Simpson to lure him to her with quiche!'

Miss Simpson and Mr Berolli. It was like a nightmare. Until today we'd never even used their names in the same sentence.

'Maybe she hypnotised him?' Ella said. 'People do weird things when they're hypnotised. This guy on TV genuinely believed he was a chicken.'

'Maybe she *drugged* him,' I suggested.

Miss Simpson had been our teacher for Food Tech since the beginning of the school year. She wasn't mean or nasty. She wasn't even that bad looking. To quote my little brother, she was just 'meh'. She was one of those teachers who have no clue how to make lessons interesting and she had even less clue how to control her class. This made Food Tech an easy doss so we'd kind of tolerated her. That was before she put the moves on Mr Berolli.

Ella shook her head, still trying to take it in. 'Miss Simpson is just so – *drippy*. And she's so *old*. And she does that weird little girly voice.'

'She's the opposite of cool,' I agreed.

We might only be fourteen but we weren't totally dumb. We knew that our love for our drama teacher could never come to anything, but we went on loving him because it made us happy. It had never bothered us that other girls in our class also had crushes on him (including the Alphas). We had never once considered them a threat. Miss Simpson was a threat and we knew it.

'Mr Berolli is *way* too young and good looking for her,' Ella said.

'It's not about looks,' Nat said fiercely. 'She and Mr Berolli are just totally wrong for each other. Mr Berolli is a lovely caring person who has been to Brazil and worked in slums and seen real suffering and she just knows about getting lumps out of white sauce!' Now Nat was almost over her shock, she was starting to get mad.

I looked at my watch. 'We're running out of time, guys, we've got twenty minutes before the end of break.'

'Better get down to business,' Ella agreed.

Nat looked blank. 'Business?'

'The Breakfast Club?' I reminded her. 'The re-launch? We're looking for a new café, remember?'

Nat covered her face. 'Sorry, sorry. I'm all over the place today.'

'Ella's drawn up a list of possible venues, haven't you, Ella?'

These were some of Ella's 'possibles': Planet Cafe, The Hill, Café Blush, Bread & Roses, the Caffeine Factory, Number 9, Sweet World Café, Café Quirk, Ting & Ting, Java Joe's, The Hummingbird Bakery, and Nat's suggestion, Books 'n' Bagels.

Nat was horrified. 'It'll take weeks to get round all those.'

'That's just like our long list,' Ella reassured her. 'We can weed some out right now. We won't have to audition them all!'

Nat pulled an apologetic face. 'Sorry, I'm being a real pain, aren't I? I do want to find a good café, truly.'

Ella and I exchanged glances. We understood Nat was still feeling fragile from her weekend, not to mention the trauma of witnessing Josh Berolli sharing Miss Simpson's quiche.

Right away we were able to rule out Java Joe's – Ella remembered they'd closed down just before Mario's. We cut out Ting & Ting and The Hummingbird Bakery. I love Ting & Ting, it has a genuinely fun vibe, but their speciality is Caribbean breakfasts and Nat is not a fan. The Hummingbird Bakery is a cute café plus their cakes are to die for, but it's pricey, also *really* small, so quickly gets packed out with designer mums and screaming toddlers. *And*, as I reminded Ella, they just do cakes and fancy types of toast and preserves, not real rib-sticking cooked breakfasts.

'What about that place round the corner from you, Ella?' I said.

'The Blue Sky Café? Good idea!' Ella added it to her list.

'We should run these past Lexie as soon as possible,' I said.

'Totally,' said Ella. 'Then we can start auditioning. Has anybody got any other suggestions?'

I shook my head.

'Nat? Hello! Earth to Natalie?' Ella said.

Nat just went on staring vacantly into space. Ella gave her a little shake and she came out of her trance with a start. 'We're not letting her get away with it,' she said abruptly. 'I won't anyway.'

'Are you still on about Josh Berolli?' said Ella.

'You bet I'm still on about him! You all agreed she's nowhere near good enough. It's . . . It's an *abomination*, that's what it is!'

'An abomination,' I repeated, giggling. 'That's harsh!'

'It's WRONG. That's why she's got to be stopped!'

We stared at her. Ella and I had seen Nat get upset loads of times but it was the first time we'd seen her hopping mad.

'Nat, we love him too,' I said. 'But what can we do?'

'"Know your enemy",' she quoted fiercely. 'That's what my great grandpa Bonneville St-John said

76

you have to do in wartime.'

'Wartime?' I echoed, bewildered.

'Yes, wartime! This is *war*, Billie, and Miss Simpson is now officially our enemy.'

To make her point, Nat angrily flattened her juice box with the palm of her hand. Unfortunately the box still had apple juice in and we all got an unexpected shower. Nat blinked away the drops as if nothing had happened. 'We are going to find out everything there is to know about Miss Simpson,' she announced. 'Unsavoury habits, deep dark secrets. If we keep searching, sooner or later we'll find something we can use against her.'

Ella had a sudden fit of the giggles. 'Unsavoury habits! Nat, you are funny.'

I didn't think Nat was being funny. I thought she was sounding totally unhinged. She abruptly stood up and I noticed that she hadn't even touched one of her sandwiches. 'So are you going to help or have I got to do it all by myself?' she demanded.

'Nat, look—' I started.

'Do you *seriously* want them to be an item, Billie? *Do* you?' she demanded.

'Of course not, but—'

'When hell freezes over,' Ella interrupted fiercely.

Nat gave a tight little nod. 'I'll do some online searches tonight. I'll find out what school she went to, then I can check out Friends Reunited for a starting point.'

'Does anyone know Miss Simpson's first name?' I asked.

Nat looked thrown. 'Actually, I don't. What about you, Ella?'

She shook her head.

'You can't do a proper search with just her surname,' I said.

'Bums.' Nat looked depressed for a moment then brightened. 'We've got her for Food Tech tomorrow. We can ask her!'

'Please, Miss Simpson, can you tell us your first name so we can find out something incriminating and ruin your love life?' I said.

'We wouldn't do it like that,' said Ella. 'We'd have to like worm our way gradually into her confidence. We can ask her innocent little questions about her school days and kind of casually get some info that way.'

I stared at my friends. 'You are SO sneaky, both of you. I'm shocked!'

I was only half joking. The idea of snooping into

Miss Simpson's private life made me genuinely uneasy. But to be honest, so did the idea of our very nearly middle-aged cookery teacher getting it on with young handsome Josh Berolli.

In fact, finding out Miss Simpson's first name was a doddle, requiring absolutely no worming on anyone's part. As we joined the other kids milling through the foyer at the end of the school day, we noticed someone had put up a new display of photographs.

The fifth and sixth years had recently put on a production of Grease, directed by Mr Berolli. The display showed highlights from rehearsals plus backstage shots with candid snaps of people who had helped out with lighting, costumes, make-up, etc. The photos had captions with the names of everyone involved. Miss Simpson had helped out with costumes: Harriet Simpson.

'*Harriet*!' said Ella in disgust. 'I might have known she'd be a Harriet!'

Just then Eddie Jones went past, shooting Ella a shy grin. Ella said, 'Oh, hiya, Eddie!' and did a princessy little wave. Ella has a *leetle* thing for Eddie, but not nearly so much of a thing as Eddie has for Ella.

'Maybe that's how the two of them got so friendly,' I

suggested. 'They got thrown together while they were working on the production.'

'She was just helping with the costumes, Billie,' Ella snapped. 'That's not exactly "working on the production".'

'We've got her name, that's the main thing.' Nat had a stubborn set to her jaw. 'I'm going on the internet the minute I get home and I'm going to dig up some dirt on that woman if I have to stay up all night.'

'Have you got to do it now?' I asked, dismayed. 'I thought we were all going round to Lexie's so we could draw up our shortlist for the auditions?'

I looked at Ella for back-up, but she pulled a face. 'Sorry, Billie. Mum said she'd be back early. We're having a girls' night in.'

Last time Ella and Annie had a girls' night in, Ella had come to school with puffy eyelids after crying herself to sleep. Her mum had intercepted a friendly text to Ella from Naomi, her dad's girlfriend, and had a major meltdown.

'You saw how Mum is,' Ella said apologetically, 'She's in a bad way. Some mornings she doesn't even put on any make-up. I thought I could give her a makeover. Not a Nellie and Plum job,' she added hastily, 'a really morale-boosting one. My mum used to look so young and pretty, Billie! People used to think we looked like sisters. I want her to take pride in herself again, you know? It's been two years since Dad left. She should be, you know . . .'

'Getting back in the mix.' I finished Ella's sentence for her, giving her hand a squeeze. 'It sounds like your mum really needs you.'

'I just want her to get back out there, you know?' For a moment Ella looked dangerously close to tears.

'You guys go home,' I told them, suppressing a sigh. 'I'll walk Bullet then I'll swing by Lexie's.'

I still had a song to write, plus my school work and two jobs to hold down, yet somehow once again I'd ended up volunteering to put in the leg-work. I'd done it because I believed we needed the Breakfast Club to get back on track. We'd only missed one Saturday but already Ella and Nat seemed to be falling apart. I didn't think we could afford to miss too many more.

I can kill two birds with one stone, I thought. I'd take Lexie her CD – that way I could see her face when she heard the special Lexie-type sounds I'd put together for her.

At least Lexie will be OK, I thought. *Lexie and me are the real tough cookies in the Breakfast Club*. And I hurried off to Mr Kaminski's.

Chapter Five

You can get to Lexie's from Ladbroke Grove by tube or a couple of buses. I decide on the bus option as the bus stop is practically outside her house.

Across the aisle, two old ladies were gossiping. Both of them had a Jamaican lilt to their voices and that Jamaican style of laughing, like the whole world is a joke, even if it's a joke that cruelly backfires now and then.

Every time I see a feisty old black lady, I think: *You could be my gran.*

Actually *my* gran wouldn't be as old as these ladies, they looked more like great grannies, but I couldn't help glancing across, enjoying their vibe.

I wish my dad had introduced us to his family. I would have made him if he'd stuck around. Mum's parents are both dead and life would have been so much better for both Mum and me if we'd had some proper family back-up after dad left. I sometimes imagine them calling us up, inviting us over for a proper Jamaican Sunday lunch: the table groaning under plates of jerk chicken, fried plantain, rice and peas, and sweet potato pie; cute little cousins running around everywhere; the older cousins cranking up the sounds.

In real life, Dad's family might not be the kind of Jamaicans I'm picturing. They might be really stuffy and work for insurance companies. I would still like to know them though. That way I'd have a real connection to my dad's past. Whatever they were like, it had to be better than a big empty hole.

My mum said that almost as soon as they met, Dad told her that he and his parents didn't get along. He said he didn't need them; he didn't need anybody except my mum. 'I suppose I thought it was quite romantic,' she confessed. Then Dad left and our little family shrank down to two and it suddenly didn't seem so romantic.

I was so caught up in my thoughts that I almost missed my stop. I scrambled to my feet and couldn't resist flashing a friendly smile at the old ladies. They smiled back; they don't always. Often they scold me, telling me I should get my hair professionally braided or I should buy some product to put on it. I have no intention of braiding my hair, plus the products they recommend are too fierce for my mix of European and Afro-Caribbean hair. Part of me wants to tell them that. Another part of me secretly likes that they feel entitled to interfere, like they think of me as a lost, slightly wayward daughter who needs correcting. Sometimes they even call me 'daughter' which makes me feel all warm inside.

I love my mixed heritage. I don't feel like I'm 'half' anything. I feel like being mixed is actually a strength, not a flaw. I wrote a song about it, actually, called *Notting Hill Girls*. It's about how years ago they had race riots in Notting Hill and politicians were predicting, like, a war between blacks and whites, but now in my time, you see girls of all colours swinging along together; beautiful, stylish, vibey girls with the wind in their hair and the world at their feet.

I realised one of the old ladies was waving at me to attract my attention. 'Zip up your bag, nuh!' she called. She pointed to my gaping bag where my purse was clearly visible.

'Too many bad people about, darlin',' her friend agreed. 'No need to mek it easy fi dem.'

85

I obediently zipped my bag. Waving my thanks to my Jamaican fairy godmothers, I jumped off the bus and ran the rest of the way to Lexie's house.

Strange boingy sounds came from the other side of their garden wall. A smooth blond head suddenly popped into view, disappearing and reappearing like a bouncing ball. One of Lexie's little brothers was playing on the trampoline.

Lexie is the only one out of all of us with a proper garden. She is also the only one whose parents are both either still alive and/or living under the same roof. Their house is what you'd call a proper family home with a mum, a dad, four kids, a dog (a rescue collie called Elvis), two cats and a steadily growing population of guinea pigs.

I used to love going to Lexie's house. When Will and Kathy first started running their business, they were in and out of the house all day long. Will said there was no point being self-employed if you couldn't choose your own hours. We'd drop round to find Will checking on his home-made wine; Kathy would cut us a slab of home-made cake she'd just taken out of the oven (healthy cake, obviously). We were in Shepherd's Bush, but it felt like we'd stepped into a country farmhouse. They even had drying herbs hanging from the ceiling.

These days just keeping the business afloat seems to be taking up all of their time, and poor Lexie always has to take up the slack. When she eventually let me in she was talking earnestly into the phone. 'I honestly don't mind, don't worry. I'm just defrosting some of that lasagne for them now. No, Clem's arm seems fine. OK, bye!' She gave me a harassed smile as she hung up. 'Hi, Billie! Sorry about that; they've got a crisis at the unit. Come through, we're in the kitchen.'

'Did I come at a bad time?' I asked anxiously.

'The total opposite!' she said, laughing. 'I'm surrounded by obnoxious little boys. I was praying to be rescued.'

I heard the microwave ping for the lasagne.

'What's wrong at the unit?' Lexie's parents rent a building on a small industrial estate where they take deliveries from suppliers and put customers' boxes of fruit and veg together.

Lexie pulled a face. 'Kathy saw a rat.'

'*Euw*,' I shuddered. 'They do say in London you're never more than three feet away from one.'

'Yeah, well, the rat man was supposed to come an hour ago, but he's held up in traffic. Sorry about the mess.'

'Don't be silly,' I said politely.

Privately I thought I'd never seen their kitchen in such total chaos. The sink was piled with dirty dishes and so were the counters. Liam was in the middle of building a complicated papier-mâché model that was taking up most of the kitchen table. From a quick glance, there looked to be more glue on Liam than there was on his model. There was wet newspaper and wire netting everywhere. The cats started winding around our ankles, demanding to be fed. Somewhere nearby, hungry guinea pigs were whistling a protest.

Clem was lying on the floor nose-to-nose with Elvis the collie, his right arm encased in plaster up to the elbow.

'What did you do this time, Clem? Fall off the trampoline?' I asked. Clem is honestly the most accident-prone kid I have ever met.

'I fell out of a tree,' he said proudly. He showed me all the autographs on his cast. 'Will did the skull and crossbones,' he said, giggling.

'Sit down, Billie,' Lexie said. 'That's if you can find a space,' she added apologetically. 'I'll give the boys their supper, then I'll make you a drink.'

I was already rolling up my sleeves. 'Looks like

you could do with a hand,' I told her. 'It'll go faster with two.'

Thirty minutes later the dishwasher was running through its cycle, the counters were washed down and cleared of clutter, Liam's model had been carefully moved into the conservatory, Cameron had come in all puffed from the trampoline and the boys were silently forking up lasagne (we had to cut Clem's up for him because of his cast). The dog, cats and guinea pigs had all been fed and Lexie and I had collapsed at the table with mugs of tea and a packet of slightly suspect wholefood biscuits we'd found in a cupboard. Lexie advised dunking them. 'They're almost edible then,' she grinned.

I puffed out my cheeks. 'How long has it been like this, Lexie?'

'Since my gran broke her hip, basically. She used to look after the boys until Kathy and Will got home. Now that she's out of action, it's mostly up to me.'

'Are you still managing to do your skating?' Skating is as crucial to Lexie as music is to me.

'Oh, God yes, don't worry! Kathy got someone to come in on skating afternoons. It's really not that bad, honestly Billie, you just caught us on a mad day!' Lexie gave me a tired smile. 'Anyway, I'm guessing you didn't come here to help me clean our disgusting kitchen?'

'Don't be daft,' I told her affectionately. 'Actually I came to bring you your birthday pressie. Sorry it's a bit late.' I handed her the CD. I'd wrapped it in pretty tissue to make it more birthdayish.

'Billie, that's so sweet! I don't know what to say!'

'I hope you like it,' I said, feeling shy.

'Thanks, Billie! I'll play it as soon as I get a moment to myself,' she promised.

'I'm also here on official Breakfast Club business.' I fished out Ella's list and pushed it over to Lexie. 'We need to know if you approve of our shortlist.'

She quickly skimmed through and pushed it back. 'Thumbs down to Books & Bagels. Apart from that, they all look good.'

'Can you think of one we've missed?'

Lexie dunked her biscuit and sucked it thoughtfully. Now she was sitting down, she was starting to look more like her usual sparkly self. 'There's a place called the Hub,' she said at last.

'Great name,' I said approvingly. 'Are you still up for checking some cafés out on Saturday?'

'You bet,' she grinned.

'We don't have to eat breakfast in each venue, obviously.'

'I could probably manage three full breakfasts! I've got a skating exam first thing.'

'First thing when?'

'Five-thirty a.m.,' she said airily.

Five-thirty in the morning sounded positively indecent to me. 'Maybe we should reschedule café auditions for the following week?'

'Don't be silly, I'll be fine. I can go home and sleep after.' Lexie dunked the rest of her biscuit and shot me a sideways look. 'So what's going on with our little Natty, does anybody know?'

I told her about Plum and Nellie's latest beauty outrage.

Lexie was horrified. 'What's wrong with them? It's not like Nat needs improving. She's gorgeous just the way she is.'

I broke the last biscuit in two and offered half to Lexie. 'Some people are bullies. That's just life.'

She pulled a face. 'I think there's something really screwy about it.' She suddenly turned on Cameron, making him and me both jump in surprise. '*Don't* feed Elvis at the table! You know what Will and Kathy would say about that.'

'Sorry, Lexie,' said Cameron, not sounding sorry in the slightest. 'I just don't happen to like lasagne that much,' he added loftily.

'Tough!' Lexie snapped. 'Lasagne is what you've got and I don't want to see any of it ending up inside the dog.'

'Don't look then,' Clem suggested mischievously.

Lexie gave him an evil glower and he quickly went back to his meal. Elvis padded around to my side of the table and fixed me with his intense collie stare.

'If Nat was someone in a story,' Lexie went on, 'the writer would make Plum and Nellie step-sisters, not *actual* sisters. But they've both joined forces with their step-mum against Nat. I mean, what is that about?'

At school, Nat occasionally let slip random scraps of info about her family situation. I shared what she'd told us with Lexie. Before she married Nat's dad, Nat's step-mum Jenny knew a lot about breeding puppies but she'd had next to nothing to do with kids. Suddenly she had two shocked little girls and a confused toddler to take care of.

'I bet Plum and Nellie were right little madams,' said Lexie.

'Plus they'd only lost their mum like a year

previously,' I reminded her. 'Nat says Plum and Nellie gave Jenny a really hard time to start with. Then she got the idea of making them into her *deputies*, making sure their naughty little sister used her potty and ate her greens and whatever.'

'The Natalie Police!' said Lexie. 'Oh, they must have *loved* that! So do you think they've just got into the habit? You've just been fed, you greedy dog!' she added, exasperated.

Elvis was wistfully resting his nose on my knee, hoping for a crumb or two of biscuit. I didn't think I should break the house rules, so I just stroked his velvety muzzle and he closed his eyes, making the best of a bad job.

'My mum has a theory,' I told Lexie. 'She says if the three of them are picking on Nat all the time, they don't need to figure out if they actually like each other. They just have to try to solve Nat.' My mum has a lot of experience of unhappy families in her job.

'Oh, no, you don't, Liam Brown!' Lexie said sharply as Liam attempted to slip away from the table. 'It's your turn to clear the dishes. The dishwasher's running, so you can stash them in the utility room.'

Liam sulkily started collecting dirty plates and cutlery, deliberately doing it in slow-motion, getting splutters of laughter from the twins.

'Take all the time you need, Liam,' I told him. 'Lexie doesn't care, do you Lex, so long as the job gets done?'

'Have you ever said any of this to Nat?' Lexie asked me. 'About the Natalie Police, I mean.'

I shook my head. I thought Nat's family situation was tricky enough without me poking my sticky fingers in.

The front door banged. 'Hi, guys! I'm back!' Will came through into the kitchen, slinging down his jacket and his messenger bag. Will always looks a bit crumpled but today he looked crumpled and incredibly tired and stressed.

He'd also lost a lot of weight, I noticed. Lexie's dad is a naturally slim person, but compared with the last time I'd seen him, his face looked really gaunt.

'Where's Kathy?' Clem whined.

'Gee thanks, Clem. I've just fought my way back across London in the rush hour but your warm welcome makes it all completely worthwhile!' There was an edge to Will's voice that showed he was genuinely hurt.

'Kathy's OK though?' Lexie asked him.

'She's fine,' Will said brusquely. 'Kathy's always fine.

I'm the grumpy pessimistic parent, according to her.'

I saw Lexie's face tighten. Will rubbed his hand across his face and tried to smile. 'No, truly she's fine. She's still waiting for the rat man. I just came back because we both thought you might need some back-up, but I see Billie's beaten me to it.'

He gave me a tired grin, then turned to the boys. 'Aren't you going to come and give your old man a hug?'

Clem suddenly stopped sulking and all three boys rushed at Will like puppies, two hanging off each arm, one on his back.

'Leave some of him for me!' Lexie joked, and she gave her dad a hug.

I suddenly felt like a spare part. Will wasn't actually being unfriendly, but he seemed super-edgy about something. I could feel that he was longing to unwind with his family after a hard day and I was in the way.

'I should be going,' I said awkwardly and picked up my bag.

'I'll give you a lift back,' Will offered. 'It's getting dark.' He meant that Ladbroke Grove is a dodgy area for a fourteen-year-old girl to be walking around by herself.

I shook my head. 'I'll be fine. It's only a couple of short bus journeys to our place.'

Lexie gave me a hug. 'Thanks for everything, Billie, and thanks for my CD.'

'I hope you like it,' I told her.

'I always love your mixes,' she said so solemnly that I could tell she really meant it. 'When you're famous I'll be boasting about you to everyone. I'll say, "I used to have breakfast with that Billie Gold every Saturday!"'

'And when you're a famous figure skater, I'll be boasting about how I used to have breakfast with that Lexie Brown!' I told her.

Going home both buses were packed. I had to stand next to some old guy with serious body odour on the second one. Five minutes is a LONG way to hold your breath, let me tell you! I was just hurrying down the street to our flat when I heard a voice say, 'It's Billie Gold! The very girl I need to see!'

I turned in surprise and saw a familiar smiling face and a glint of a gold tooth. 'Dino! How's it going?'

'A lot better now I seen you, Miss Gold. You lookin' pert!'

I looked down at my crumpled school uniform and

spluttered with laughter. 'Yeah, right!'

'Serious, man! You look good. In fact right now you're looking like my guardian angel.'

Like a lot of young people round Ladbroke Grove, Dino has to juggle several different jobs to make a living. He helps out a couple of guys on the market, does a spot of security work, plus some DJing on the side, and he does little building jobs for his cousin who runs a company called Local Hero (No Job Too Small).

I narrowed my eyes and gave Dino my look. 'Let me guess. You need me to cover for you at Vaughan's record stall.'

He grinned. 'Can't put anything past you, princess! The minute I saw your face I felt this light bulb flash on in my brain. I'm like, "Oho! Maybe Miss Gold will take pity on you and help you out!"'

I sighed. 'When do you need cover?'

'From three to five tomorrow.' I noticed Dino was carefully avoiding my eyes.

'Tomorrow! Jeez, you really *do* need a guardian angel!' I puffed out my cheeks. 'I still have to go to school, you know.'

'Three-thirty then? Only my girlfriend is kicking off because I haven't been over to see her and Tiego for a

97

while.' Tiego was Dino's little boy.

When I didn't answer, Dino said desperately, 'Three forty-five then? If I got you covering for me, Vaughan won't mind me swapping shifts. You might only be fifteen but he knows you know your music, innit?'

'For the record, Dino, I'm fourteen,' I corrected.

He did an exaggerated double-take. 'Are you *serious*, baby girl? You are *way* too cool and sophisticated to be only fourteen.'

Dino was just sweet-talking me to get himself out of a jam. I knew it and he knew it. Dino should seriously include, 'Charms birds out of the trees' on his CV. If he put his mind to it, I bet he could even charm miserable Mrs Gildersleeve.

'Go on then,' I sighed. 'Give me your mobile number. I'm not promising anything, OK?'

I could maybe ask one of Mr Kaminski's neighbours to walk Bullet as a one-off. I fished out my gel pen and Dino wrote his number on my palm. Flirtily hanging on to my hand, he peered more closely at his handwriting. 'It's all sparkly,' he said amused.

Not looking so cool and sophisticated now, Billie, I thought.

'OK, Miss Gold, I'll be waiting for your call,' Dino said. 'Later, yeah?'

I walked away grinning. I'd be earning money doing something music-related. Also I liked working on Vaughan's stall. The first time I'd stood in for Dino, Vaughan had followed me about like a worried puppy, terrified I was going to inflict major damage on his precious vinyl.

Then I said casually, 'Oh, wow, you've got My Guy by Mary Wells!' and his jaw just dropped.

'You've *heard* of Mary Wells?'

I'd found the key to Vaughan's heart. Motown! Like Mitch, he was a fanatic. He had thousands of old Motown records: Martha and the Vandellas, the Four Tops, the Supremes, Smoky Robinson and the Miracles, Gladys Knight and the Pips. Once Vaughan realised I was a genuine fan, his worried puppy expression vanished and never came back. 'Good to know I come in useful,' Mitch joked when I told him.

Before I put my key in the lock, something made me step back and peep in through our window. The kitchen blind was up and all the lights were on, making it glow with a friendly yellow light. Mum was sitting at the table. She'd got her new reading glasses on as she went through some case notes. Finlay ran up to show her something and she looked up, smiling.

Mitch had his back to me so I could see his bald head shining. He was wearing a stripy butcher's apron, busily chopping something. If Mitch was cooking we'd be having macaroni cheese, spaghetti and meatballs or chilli. These are the three main dishes Mitch knows (not counting pancakes). Finlay ran past my mum holding his toy high over his head, making it zoom around the room. It was the yellow plane I'd given him for his birthday. *He'll be making irritating aeroplane noises*, I thought. Little boys were SO weird.

I watched them for a moment, enjoying the picture they made. Then I heard a familiar yowl and something rubbed up against my legs.

'Oh, you're back are you, you little stop-out?'

Our cat, Sparkle, has lived with us since the night Mitch found her scared and starving down near the skate park. Her full name (chosen by Finlay) is Sparkle Tiger. She's a proper pedigree Bengal tiger cat, with tiger-striped fur that actually sparkles in the light. Mitch advertised on all the Bengal tiger cat websites to see if anyone had reported her missing. No one had. She still has a tendency to go walkabout, and often goes missing for days, but so far, cross fingers, she has always come back.

I held the door open for her while she decided

whether to come in. Sparkle is beautiful but not terribly bright. 'Come on, Sparks, make up your mind,' I told her.

She strolled ahead of me, tail waving.

'IS THAT YOU BILLIE?' Finlay shouted from the kitchen.

'It's me and Sparks and we're both starvin' like Marvin!'

I walked towards the smell and sizzle of frying onions and spices. I was hungry and happy. It was to be my last normal day for a while.

Chapter Six

It started with a dream.

I call it my 'mystery dream'. I've been having it forever – well, ever since I started to think of myself as a singer. Basically the dream goes like this. I'm in a club waiting to go on stage. In the dream my dad is still alive. He's already on stage playing. The only recognisable people in the dream are my dad playing his beautiful sax, and me, waiting. The people at the tables, the other musicians, are all somehow out of focus as if I'm seeing them through clouds of dry ice, like the dream is telling me they don't really count.

My dad starts playing the riff that is my cue to run on and join him, but before I can move, a mysterious woman in a glittering cocktail dress softly slips past me. She immediately starts singing a duet with my dad's sax and, this is the first weird thing, it's *my* song that she's singing. She sings it differently to how I'd do it. I guess it's the difference between a girl and a grown woman. But her interpretation is amazing. The other weird thing is I'm not jealous. I just feel an overwhelming longing to see the face of the singer who's singing my song, but I always wake up before I get the chance.

This time though, something was different. As the mystery woman slipped past, she put something into my hand: an old-style cassette.

I woke up in the almost dark, feeling doubly spooked, as the weirdness of my dream crashed into my usual early-morning scary-hole sensations. If I could have brought that dream cassette with me back into real life and actually played it, what would I have heard? I didn't need to ask the question. I knew. I'd hear my dad playing his sax.

The haunting atmosphere of my dream stayed with me as I showered, dressed and sleepwalked into the kitchen to join my family's early morning kitchen dance: pouring orange juice, grabbing a bite of toast, half an eye on the clock.

Mitch was trying to get Finlay to finish his cereal. 'Five minutes then we're going, so eat up, dude, OK?' he warned.

'I'm not actually in the mood for cereal.' Finlay pushed his plate away.

My mum was wearing her social worker clothes: a navy blue suit with a crisp white blouse that made her look like a stranger. She was frowning at herself in the kettle. Part of her fringe was sticking up and she was trying to pat it into position.

'We don't still have any old cassettes, do we?' I tried to sound casual.

'Unlikely. Has anyone seen my specs?' Mum started hunting around, not looking at me.

'We used to have one though, right?' I said. Something was nudging at my memory. 'I thought I saw one quite recently?'

'No one uses cassettes now.' Mum looked distracted. 'Mitch, have you seen my glasses? I can't have lost them *already*!'

She started scanning the kitchen in an agitated sort of way. It's not like her to get in a state over such a little thing.

'Nina! Calm down, woman, they're here!' Mitch held up her specs, grinning. 'They were in the fruit bowl.'

My step-dad planted a kiss on my head, picked up his car keys and headed for the door with my little brother in tow. I heard Finlay say plaintively:

'Daddy, I don't actually feel very well.'

'You say that every morning, Finlay, and as soon as you see your friends you feel totally fine.'

As they left the flat I could still hear Finlay whingeing.

While Bullet and I did our little morning circuit, I mentally replayed the conversation with my mum.

For the first few years after my dad left, Mum and I lived in a poky little studio flat. In such a cramped space there is nowhere for you to hide, so I *know* my mum; and I know when she isn't being a hundred per cent truthful.

When I asked her about the cassette, I didn't see her face but I got this, like, weird Polaroid flash inside my head and I knew that Mum and I were both seeing the same cluttered drawer stuffed with all kinds of random objects she hadn't been able to bring herself to throw away: things like a ball of tangled string or an old broken cassette. The cassette was real and it was somewhere in our flat. I knew it. Mum knew it. So why would she lie?

I screwed up my face, trying to remember. There had been an odds and ends drawer in our old wobbly-legged kitchen table. Then a couple of years ago, Mum and Mitch went to Ikea and bought a brand-new table without a drawer. I seemed to remember that Mum had put our old table on Freecycle, but I had no idea what she'd done with the odds and ends from the drawer.

Like I said, I know my mum pretty well and I know that despite everything, she'd never once regretted loving my dad. It would be just like her to keep a tape of him playing his sax, even though the tape was broken and useless. She'd keep it because throwing away my dad's music would be like she was throwing the best part of my dad away and she couldn't do that.

On the other hand, she'd never dream of mending it because – well, I already told you how my mum feels about music.

On the way back to Mr Kaminski's, Bullet and I took a little detour to Mrs Salazar's flat. Mrs Salazar is an old friend of Mr Kaminski's. To my relief she said she was happy to walk Bullet any time I got stuck.

I texted Dino right away. cu @ pbello 3.30.

I had a ton of stuff to lug to school that morning: my games things, ingredients for Food Tech (we were making lemon meringue pie) and a pair of clean jeans, a T-shirt and hoodie for changing into after school. I didn't think Vaughan would like me to turn up to work in school uniform.

Nat caught me up outside school.

'Hi, girl!' I gave her a beaming smile. 'How's Betty?'

She beamed back. 'She's SOO cute!'

'And how did you get on with your searches?'

'I didn't,' said Nat. 'You would not *believe* how many people in this country are called Harriet Simpson.'

'Hey, at least you tried,' I told her.

Nat looked shocked. 'I'm still going ahead with it, Billie! I'm a Bonneville, and we don't give up. I need more info, that's all.'

We were in the playground now in a jostling crush of blue and grey uniforms. Fareeda suddenly separated herself out of the crush.

'GRRR! I could kill Alice!' she growled.

'Yeah? Hussey or Hobbs?' I said.

'Hussey.' Fareeda almost spat out the name.

'We all hate Alice Hussey,' said Nat cheerfully. 'What's she done this time?'

Fareeda rolled her eyes. 'I told her my cousin and I got tickets to see JLS and immediately she's like, "Oh, did you *reeeally*? Me and my friend actually *talked* to them backstage."'

It was a brilliant imitation and Nat and I both laughed.

'If you'd told Alice Hussey you'd met JLS backstage she'd have said, "Oh, did you *reeeally*?"' I told Fareeda. '"Me and my friend actually *snogged* them!"'

'Back in a sec,' said Nat suddenly, 'I just need to talk to Oliver.'

Nat zoomed over to a cute-faced boy with short curly hair. Ella and I refer to him as NNB, as in Not Nat's Boyfriend. 'Yes, Oliver is my friend and he is a boy but he is Not My Boyfriend, OK!' she snapped once when we were teasing her. 'Poor Oliver,' Ella sighed later when the two of us were alone. 'He's totally crushing on Nat but she *totally* can't see it.'

When Nat is not a) with us or b) at home being tortured by Plum and Nellie, you will usually find her hanging out with Oliver Maybury. (Not 'Ollie', Nat is very clear on that point. 'His name is *Oliver*, OK?')

Oliver is a sweetheart; he's really tall, and really funny – in an understated kind of way. He's also scarily bright. Nat says in a movie he'd be the teenager who knew how to hack into the Pentagon. I watched her explaining something to him, making gestures as she talked (Nat is a great arm waver), then I felt someone touch me on the shoulder and there was Ella beaming at me.

'Hiya! How's you? Did you see Lexie?'

I nodded. 'She totally approved of our café shortlist. She also suggested the Hub.'

'Ooh, I like the sound of the Hub,' said Ella. 'And how was our lovely Lexie?'

I told her about Lexie having to hold the fort at home now her gran was out of action. Then I told her about Dino asking me to help out on Vaughan's stall after school.

The moment I mentioned Dino, Ella did that funny little thing she does with her nostrils, like she'd got a whiff of something nasty. 'Isn't Dino that guy who has fathered, like, three little kids with different girls?'

'Ella, I'm just helping out on a stall, OK? I'm not having Dino's fourth child.'

My voice came out sharper than I meant and Ella blinked in surprise. 'I was just *saying*!' she said. 'No need to bite my head off.'

'Yes there is a need, actually,' I told her fiercely.

'You've just made this instant assumption that Dino's a bad person. He's not. He's just a typical guy from the Grove.'

'You live in the Grove,' Ella pointed out. 'I doubt you'll have three kids by the time you're nineteen.'

'No, because I've got a mum and step-dad who actually care about me. Dino and his brothers virtually had to bring themselves up. At least Dino tries to be a good dad to his kids, which is more than his dad did for him!'

I saw Ella swallow. The self-righteous expression had been totally wiped off her face. 'I didn't know that,' she admitted humbly. 'I shouldn't go shooting my mouth off. I'm sorry, Billie.'

That is one thing I love about Ella. She might get up on her high horse, but when she realises she's wrong, she hops down in a heartbeat.

I quickly changed the subject. 'Have you heard if they've got Kitty's little Nikes yet?'

'Not yet. You only posted them on Monday though.'

I was feeling bad for snapping at Ella. It isn't her fault she's lived such a protected life. She never had to live in one room surviving on baked-bean soup like me and Mum, or go nicking in Iceland to put food on the table like Dino and his brothers. Ella and I lived in the same city, but we had lived in completely different worlds. She was also my oldest friend. I hooked my arm through hers to show I was sorry. 'So how was your girly night in?'

Her face clouded. 'Oh, that didn't actually happen. Mum's friend, the one that's getting a divorce, phoned up in a right state so Mum told her to come round and they holed up in the kitchen drinking Chardonnay and slanging off their exes.'

'Sounds like a lot of fun for you,' I said. 'Not!'

Ella spluttered with laughter. 'You are wicked, you know that?'

'Not so wicked as we're going to be!' Nat had reappeared. She flashed a fiendish grin. 'Food Tech this afternoon, when we turn the spotlight on – durn, durn, durn – Miss Harriet Simpson!'

Ella rubbed her hands. 'Fun, fun, fun.'

I am not a major fan of Miss Simpson but it was faintly disturbing to see my friends so totally out for trouble, especially Nat. I've seen Ella take against teachers before. But I'd always thought of Nat as a genuinely kind person. This situation with Mr Berolli was bringing out a side I never knew existed.

* * *

It turned out Nat couldn't wait until the afternoon to start making mischief. At the end of double drama, when we were all hanging back to talk to (i.e. flirt with) Mr Berolli, she blurted out:

'Sir, can I ask you something? What do you think about women who go out with much younger men, sir? Do you think they're disgusting cradle snatchers, or are they just, like, really sick, deluded and sad?' There was a strange gleam in her eyes that I'd never seen before.

Mr Berolli would have made a brilliant actor. You could hardly tell he'd been thrown off-balance. He looked thoughtful for a moment then he said smoothly, 'Interesting bit of improv work, Miss Bonneville-St John, but our drama session actually finished five minutes ago and you should all be making your way quickly and quietly to your next lesson.'

Nat is not such a bad actor herself. She instantly slipped back into schoolgirl mode. 'OK, sir, see you later sir,' she said meekly.

In Food Tech, she and Ella waited so long to make their move I thought they must have chickened out. I was secretly relieved. I enjoy cooking, so I was happy to just concentrate on making my pastry shell and preparing the lemon filling for the pie.

Finlay loves it when I bring home dishes I've made in Food Tech and he's especially mad about lemon meringue pie.

Now and then I heard Nat and Ella whispering.

'What is she *thinking* of, wearing that dress?'

'Somebody probably told her vintage was in!'

'Then they should have explained that vintage doesn't mean old and manky. That green is *soo* unflattering.'

'I know! Looks like she found it in a pond!'

There was also whispering going on between Tamsin and the Alphas.

'Now I've started you off, do you want to take over rolling your pastry?' Tamsin said encouragingly.

'No,' pouted Pia. 'You finish. I will only break nail.'

The Alphas have maids to do everything for them at home (or so they like to make out) so they have never learned even the most basic skills, and I mean *basic*: for instance, how to boil an egg. Being Alphas though, they try to give the impression that being useless in the kitchen is, in fact, a highly desirable quality.

Oliver is one of the few boys who does Food Tech, and week after week he had watched in disbelief as Miss Simpson totally let the Alphas get away with it. It was when Tamsin started briskly whipping Danni's egg whites for her that he finally cracked.

'Miss Simpson,' he asked politely. 'Do you really think it's OK for Pia and the others to use Tamsin as their unpaid servant?'

At this point I should explain that Tamsin and Nat actually have something quite surprising in common. They are both really fond of Oliver (Not Nat's Boyfriend) Maybury. Admittedly with Tamsin, it's more of a hopeless crush. Oliver was the first person to be nice to her when she came to our school and I think she has secret hopes that one day he might actually ask her to be his GF.

Now Oliver had spoken up for her in public, she went totally pink up to her ears. Then one of the Alphas gave a warning little cough and Tamsin quickly pulled herself together.

'I don't mind helping them, Miss Simpson,' she said, flustered.

'You see?' Isabella said sweetly. 'Tamsin is happy. We are all very happy. There is not a problem.' She shot Oliver a murderous look.

I think Oliver had shamed Miss Simpson into finally taking control of her class, because she now bravely insisted that the Alphas had to beat their own egg whites.

'But I got weak *wrist*!' Pia flapped her arms pathetically like little broken wings to demonstrate how weak.

'Then just do the best you can.'

Miss Simpson actually sounded unusually firm for Miss Simpson. Pia said something rude in Russian (or maybe it just sounded rude) and the other Alphas all looked daggers at Miss Simpson.

At last, all the lemon meringue pies were in the ovens with their meringue crusts turning pale gold and crispy. Everyone did the cleaning up, except the Alphas who ignored their eggy/lemony bowls and utensils and sat chatting to each other in their usual confusing mix of French, English and Russian. We could see Miss Simpson trying to decide if she had the energy to force them to do their own dirty work for the umpteenth time or if it was just simpler to do it herself.

Ella and Nat exchanged looks.

'Don't worry, Miss Simpson, we'll help you,' Ella said.

Miss Simpson eagerly took the bait. 'That's really kind,' she said in her girly but rather grating voice.

Nat, Ella and I quickly formed an efficient human chain, with Miss Simpson doing the washing up and Nat, me and Ella drying and putting away.

I saw Nat give Ella another meaningful look. Miss Simpson didn't know it, but she had just jumped from the frying pan into the fire.

'Miss,' Nat said innocently, 'my friends and I were wondering if you always wanted to be a teacher, Miss?'

Miss Simpson looked startled. Until today we had shown no interest in her whatsoever. Now we had not only volunteered to help her, we were talking to her as if she was a real human being. She gave a shy little laugh.

'Actually, when I was growing up I wanted to be a vet.'

'So did you have one teacher that you, like, really admired, Miss?' asked Ella. She made her eyes all soft and kittenish; a kitten with hidden claws.

'I did have one teacher that I admired, yes,' said Miss Simpson.

'Was he a drama teacher?' Ella said, quick as a flash.

'Yes, because you've got a bit of a thing for drama teachers, haven't you, Miss?' Nat said, not quite under her breath.

A puzzled crinkle appeared on Miss Simpson's forehead. I could tell she was wondering if she'd heard that quite right.

'So where did you actually grow up, Miss?' Ella went on, pretending Nat hadn't said anything.

'In the midlands,' said Miss Simpson, 'just outside Leicester. I went to a girls' convent.'

She was giving away too much, too easily, I thought.

Nat gave her a little smirk. 'You went to a convent! Did you want to be a nun, Miss?'

'Oh, dear, no, I don't think I'd have been at all successful as a nun,' Miss Simpson said without thinking.

Nat and Ella broke into broad grins.

'REALLY, Miss?' said Ella. 'Were you a bit of a goer then?'

For the first time, Miss Simpson looked flustered. 'Not at all, but to be a nun you have to be extremely devout.'

'Plus the clothes aren't that flattering, are they, Miss.' Ella put on a sympathetic face.

'Yes, Miss, you wouldn't be able to wear a nice dress like that,' Nat said. 'I think I saw it last week, Miss, in the Oxfam shop? Is that where you bought it?'

Miss Simpson was starting to look trapped and upset. 'Actually, I think it's time to check on our—'

Ella swiftly headed her off. 'So when you decided

not to be a vet and you thought you'd rather be a teacher, what exactly made you decide to be a cookery teacher?'

Nat didn't wait for Miss Simpson to answer. 'I bet you've had a lot of boyfriends, haven't you, Miss? Were any of them really famous? I could see Miss with someone really famous, couldn't you, Billie?'

I didn't want to be dragged into this spiteful little game. I wished Nat and Ella had never started it, but I didn't know a way to make it stop so I just mumbled something.

'What about a celebrity chef, Miss?' That funny little gleam was back in Nat's eyes. 'You could sit up all night discussing your favourite recipes together, or do you just only fancy *drama* teachers, Miss?'

Miss Simpson looked like a panicky rabbit now, caught in Nat and Ella's merciless headlights. I felt genuinely sorry for her. Then for the second time that afternoon, Oliver saved the day.

'Miss Simpson, can I smell burning?'

There was a mad rush to the cookers to rescue our lemon meringues (apart from the Alphas, who just sauntered). We still had ten minutes to go 'til home time, but the spell had been broken and Nat and Ella knew it. Gabbling something about playground duty, Miss Simpson scuttled out of the classroom as if she couldn't wait to get away, leaving us to pack up our lemon meringue pies.

Oliver hovered solicitously as Nat struggled to fit the tin with her lemon meringue pie on the top of the madly disorganised contents in her bag. You could see he was desperate to take over and do it properly.

'Maybe you should repack it and start again,' he suggested tentatively.

'Isn't there somewhere you've got to be, Oliver?' Nat said, looking irritated. 'Don't you usually go to see that private tutor after Food Tech?'

'I do,' Oliver admitted, blushing. 'But you look like you need some help.'

'Well, I don't,' she snapped.

'OK,' he said calmly. 'Guess I'll see you tomorrow then.' He turned back at the classroom door to see if Nat was watching but she had already gone into a huddle with Ella.

'We went to all that trouble and she didn't even give us any juicy info,' Ella pouted.

Nat grinned. 'Hey, it was fun. Anyway, I've thought of a better plan.'

Oh God, what? I thought.

That strange gleam was back in her eyes. 'You know

what they say? A picture is worth a thousand words!'

'What picture? What are you talking about?'

Nat tapped her nose. 'Wait and see.'

'You were very quiet this afternoon, Billie,' Ella said, glancing at me.

'I'm feeling quiet,' I told them. 'I'm having a quiet day.' And I picked up my tin with my lemon meringue pie and left.

Chapter Seven

I flew into the girls' toilets and quickly changed into my real clothes. I unfastened my hair clip, letting my curls fall loose around my shoulders and gave my reflection a cool stare. 'You look way too cool and sophisticated to be only fourteen,' I told myself. I stretched out the corners of my eyelids, pulling a hideous face. 'Yeah, right!'

I jogged most of the way to Portobello, knowing Dino would be looking anxiously at his watch. The sun was shining and people's window boxes were full of spring flowers. I was out and about in my favourite city and though the scene with Miss Simpson had left a bad taste, I felt my spirits gradually lift.

There aren't that many stalls on Portobello Market on week days, it's mostly just where local people buy fruit and veg. There were just a couple of antique stalls and a scattering of clothes stalls. Vaughan's Vinyl was sandwiched between a stall selling vintage comics and a mad clothes stall run by some design students. I ran up and tapped Dino on the shoulder.

'You can go now,' I told him breathlessly.

He did an exaggerated double-take. 'Miss G! You here already! You're ten minutes early, man!'

Dino was sharply dressed in designer jeans, a dazzling white T-shirt and a butter-smooth leather jacket. He'd dressed up to impress his girlfriend, I thought. Dino hunted through the pictures on his phone and showed me a photo of Tiego eating something mushy and green.

'He looks like a real cutie,' I said.

He waggled his eyebrows. 'You know what they say, Miss G. Like father like son!'

Vaughan coughed. 'I'll serve this customer, shall I?'

I have no idea how old Vaughan is. His face has that uncooked-dough look that overweight people sometimes get. He was wearing his usual shapeless jacket in a shade of beige you couldn't imagine anyone deliberately choosing, and an ancient pair of trainers. His hair needed a good cut. If anyone in Notting Hill needed a makeover, it was Vaughan.

'So how's the songwriting going?' he asked me when

both Dino and the customer had gone. 'Working on anything new?'

'Kind of,' I said shyly. I don't like to talk about my songs until they're finished.

The first hour was really slow. Dino says Vaughan only does Portobello Market on week days because he doesn't have a life. But if you ask me, Motown *is* Vaughan's life. He doesn't have a girlfriend (or a boyfriend) as far as I know. He doesn't even have a cat. He saves all his passion for Motown.

There were a surprising number of people about for a week day, mostly American tourists. Like always, one came up to ask if we could direct her and her husband to the cute travel book store that featured in the movie *Notting Hill*. Vaughan rolled his eyes and left her to me.

I tried to explain that the real shop was around the corner in Blenheim Crescent, just off Portobello. The shop they used for the movie wasn't a bookshop; it was an antique shop. When the antique shop closed down it was turned into a furniture store, then more recently it had become a shoe shop.

I could see she wasn't taking it in. She and her husband set off on their quest looking so excited I had the feeling they actually expected to find Hugh Grant behind the counter with Julia Roberts going, 'I'm just a girl in love with a boy.'

No one stopped at the stall after that, even for directions, so Vaughan went to get us both a hot drink. It was the first time I'd been left in charge and I felt ridiculously proud.

After a few minutes, a guy came strolling casually by. I noticed him because he was wearing what I immediately thought of as a blues singer's hat. It wasn't the actual hat, which was a Trilby – more the way he wore it that made me think he must be some kind of musician. It was hard to tell how old he was: not young, perhaps around the age my dad would be if he was alive.

These thoughts were flashing through my mind at the speed of light when the man apparently changed his mind about something. Retracing his steps, he walked straight up to our stall.

'Have you got anything by Jimmie Logan?' he asked, not quite looking me in the eye.

I'd helped on Vaughan's stall maybe four or five times now and no one has EVER asked me for anything by my dad. This is not surprising. Motown was well before my dad's day; also, my dad never made any commercial recordings so far as I know.

I was so shocked I couldn't answer him at first.

'Actually, we more specialise in sixties and seventies music,' I managed at last. My heart was beating so hard I thought I was going to faint. 'Vaughan, the guy who owns this stall, will be back soon. If you don't mind waiting, he might be able to help.'

'You heard of him though, yeah?' said Blues Hat with a sideways look. 'You heard of Jimmie Logan?'

I tried to make my voice more normal. 'I know he was supposed to be a good sax player.'

'No *supposed* about it,' he said sharply. 'Jimmie was the best.'

I could see Vaughan approaching, carrying two brimming plastic cups. I swallowed. My heart rate was slowing down but I still felt weirdly light-headed. I wasn't sure if this was even happening.

'You actually knew—' I almost said 'my dad,' then quickly covered my slip. 'You actually knew him?'

Blues Hat laughed a gravelly kind of laugh. '*Knew* him! Jimmie and me were practically brothers.' He turned to go.

'Wait!' I said in a panic. 'Have you got a card or something? What's your name?'

He gave me his sharp humorous look. 'Just an old friend from the past, that's all. I can see you're growing up fine, Billie, really fine. Your mother made the right decision.' And he strolled off, just glancing back once and touching his hat, leaving me spinning. Blues Hat had called me by my name.

Vaughan handed me my drink. 'What did he want?'

'You did see him then? You saw that guy in the hat?' I was afraid I'd somehow made him up.

He snorted. 'Yeah, I saw him. Looked like someone out of *The Blues Brothers*.'

'Have you seen him before?'

'Never seen him in my life,' said Vaughan, taking a slurp of his tea. 'I assume he didn't want directions to Hugh Grant's travel bookshop?'

'He wanted to know if we had any records by Jimmie Logan.' It was hard to say my dad's name. *But that was just an excuse*, I thought. *He knew who I was, he knew my mum.*

'Who's Jimmie Logan?' asked Vaughan.

'My dad,' I told him.

'Your dad made records? I didn't know that.'

'That's it. I don't think he did.'

Vaughan laughed. 'You do realise you're not making any sense?'

That could be because my entire *life* wasn't making sense.

A man who claimed to be a friend of my dad's had

turned up out of the blue, a man who knew about me and my mum. And what did he mean: my mum made the right choice?

Walking home, I was totally wired. It had been a disturbing day from start to finish. I had woken from a recurring dream about an unknown woman, witnessed Nat, one of my kindest friends, on some kind of search-and-destroy mission, been accosted by a strange man, and then there was the mystery cassette.

When I got home, I found that Mitch and Finlay had been back for hours. For once my little brother hadn't been faking his symptoms. He'd been taken ill at school. Mum was in a meeting so Mitch had gone to fetch him home. He was now tucked up on the sofa listlessly watching *Rasta Mouse*. Sparks was curled up loyally beside him, with one watchful amber eye half open.

'Glad to see you've got your Sparkle Tiger looking after you,' I said.

'She knows I'm not very well that's why.' Finlay leaned his face against his beloved cat and closed his eyes.

'What's up with him?' I asked Mitch.

He shrugged. 'Temperature. Nasty cough. Probably just a bug.'

'Mitch, do you know what happened to all the things we used to keep in the old table drawer: the spare keys and whatever?'

My step-dad sighed. 'You haven't lost your door key *again*?'

'It's not the keys, there are some things I haven't seen since Mum gave away our table. I wanted to check that they haven't been thrown away.'

'Most things in this flat end up in Finlay's room, I find,' said Mitch, ruffling my little brother's hair. 'Like Daddy's wind-up torch, eh, buddy?'

Instead of doing his mischievous high-pitched giggle, Finlay let out a pathetic wail. 'I didn't mean to, Daddy!' That's when I realised he really was poorly.

Mum called to check how Finlay was doing and Mitch followed her instructions, cooling him with damp flannels, giving him baby aspirin. We changed him into fresh PJs, then I read Finlay a story while Mitch started on the evening meal.

In the middle of *The Tiger Who Came to Tea*, my phone beeped. I managed to squint at my mobile without interrupting the story. It was a text from Jools asking me to call her. 'Shan't be a minute, Fin,' I told him. 'I just need to talk to a friend.'

It was less than three weeks since I'd seen Jools at

Mario's but it felt like a lifetime since I'd heard her warm husky voice. 'Hi Jools, what's up?'

'I've got some news,' said Jools. 'Our fundraiser for Freya is still going ahead. We've been lucky enough to get a free venue. I wanted to know if you'd still be willing to sing?'

'I'd— oh, wow – I'd love to, Jools.'

'You don't sound too sure,' she said.

'No, I am!' I pulled myself together. 'I'm surprised, that's all. I thought it was all off.'

'No way,' Jools said fiercely. 'Freya should be running around like other kids her age. I want to help make that happen.'

'So where's the venue?'

'Oh, the Grove,' she said casually as if it was no biggie to have secured the coolest club in West London.

'You got the Grove for free? That's *amazing*, Jools! You must be a really persuasive lady.'

She laughed her husky laugh. 'I've had a lot of practice!'

We arranged to meet up at the Grove the next day after I'd walked Bullet, so we could talk through my set. I was really happy that the fundraiser was still going ahead. What worried me was how I was going to persuade my mum. I should really have asked her when Jools first approached me to sing, but I'd chickened out. I told myself I'd get it over with tonight, but the moment my mum walked through the door, all I could think of was Blues Hat's voice saying: *Your mother made the right choice.*

That night I sat with Mum and Mitch trying to watch a show on TV, one I usually love, but it was just white noise.

'I'm having an early night,' I told my mum abruptly. 'I didn't sleep well last night.'

There was a wail from Finlay's room. My mum went running.

'I'm not sure any of us is going to sleep too well tonight either,' Mitch sighed.

As soon as I was alone in my room, I went straight to my dad's photo. I stared and stared at it as if I could somehow melt my way through the picture to the real Jimmie Logan. Suddenly I found myself picturing the man in the hat. I went back to the photograph then screwed my eyes tight shut, summoning up Blues Hat's features and expression, trying to make them match. You're mad, I told myself. *Just because he's the right age, he's a musician and he's black doesn't mean he's your dad.*

I plopped down hard on my bed, then immediately jumped up again and started to pace. I was jangling with excitement and nerves, a crazy gleam of hope somewhere in the mix. It had been ten years. He'd have changed. A person can change a lot in ten years.

Not that much, I argued with myself. If a daughter came face to face with her long-lost dad she'd recognise him, even after ten years. Wouldn't she?

Mum had always said my dad was dead. Was she telling the truth? Was I crazy to dream, to *imagine* . . .

I was tugging at my hair. I was shaking. I thought my head was going to explode.

If my dad wasn't dead, where had he been all these years? If he wasn't dead, why had he never tried to find me 'til now? Most of all, if he wasn't dead why had Mum told me he was?

I'm going crazy, I thought. *This kind of thing doesn't happen in real life.*

I took deep, slow breaths until I'd almost stopped trembling. Now I was just really, *really* cold. I needed a hot drink or I'd never sleep.

I went to make myself a hot chocolate. On my way back to my room, I noticed Finlay's door standing partly open. I could see Mum bending over him in the glow of his old Night Garden lamp that he still adores.

She saw me and put her finger to her lips, letting me know Finlay had finally dropped off to sleep. I tiptoed softly past to show I understood, but the weirdness that had sprung up between us this morning was still there.

My mother was not a liar. She was the most honest person I'd ever met. When I was five, I stole a strawberry off a market stall when I thought she wasn't looking. My mum actually made me go up to the owner of the stall with my little five-year-old knees knocking and confess.

I went back to my room and sat up in bed sipping hot chocolate and waiting for the weirdness to go away. I waited and waited but it didn't happen.

Chapter Eight

I t wasn't even light when I woke. For some reason
my brain had switched on. I sometimes get ideas for
songs in my sleep. I wake and they're just there waiting,
as if someone delivered them in the night. This morning
I didn't have an idea for a song, and for once, miracle
of miracles, I didn't wake up to the scary-hole feeling.
But I *had* remembered what happened to the stuff in
the kitchen-table drawer.

It was only 5 a.m. In two hours I'd have to get up
and go to school, but somehow today that didn't matter.
Something was pulling me out of bed and along the
corridor into the box room where Mitch keeps his
vintage vinyl. There's also an old desk where he and
mum take care of household bills. The desk has a
drawer, but the cassette wasn't in there. I knew exactly
where it was.

I got down on my hands and knees and crawled right under the desk until I could see the miniature chest of drawers that has travelled with my mum and me to every place we've ever lived since Dad left us. The chest started out natural wood colour. We decided this was way too dull, so we painted the drawers all wild colours. Each drawer was full of different kinds of junk: coiled cables from who knows what electronic equipment, old mobile chargers, rubber bands, sets of Allen keys, drawing pins, a teeny pack of cards out of a Christmas cracker. I carefully pulled out drawer after drawer. The cassette was in the last, smallest, flamingo-pink drawer. I snatched it up and dashed back to my room, my heart beating like a drum.

It's my dad, I told myself angrily. *I have a right*.

Safely back in bed, I turned over the cracked cassette case. There was no writing on the case, no clue to what was on the tape. I slipped the cassette out of its box. Like I'd remembered, the brown plastic tape was hanging out in loops. I fished in my bedside drawer until I found a pencil and used it to rewind the tape until it all fitted tightly back inside the cassette. It might not work. The tape might be too damaged. I wouldn't know until I played it.

There is a cassette player in our house. It's built into

an ancient mini stereo that we keep in the kitchen for dancing around to while we're cooking. The kitchen, the least private place in our flat. I'd have to wait until everyone was out. Now Finlay was so poorly, I might be waiting a while. I tucked the cassette away tenderly in my bedside drawer.

At last it was officially time to get up. I trudged around the block with wheezy little Bullet, came home, gulped half a glass of juice, nibbled the corner off a piece of toast, then went to say goodbye to my mum who had taken the day off work to look after Finlay. He was wrapped up in his quilt, watching *Dora the Explorer*, looking like a tiny ghost, if ghosts wore dinosaur pyjamas.

'You're not looking too great either, Billie,' Mum commented. 'I hope you're not going down with Finlay's bug?'

'I'm fine,' I said.

And our eyes collided and there it was again, that unmistakable weirdness. *Your mother made the right choice.*

What choice? The inside of my head felt like those loops of tape hanging out of the broken cassette. If only there was a way to rewind it so things made sense.

* * *

I can't tell you one thing that occurred during the first two lessons. But at break something happened that snapped me almost back to normal.

Nat caught up with me and Ella in the playground. She was carrying one of those large plastic wallets, the kind that super-organised people like my step-dad use to keep papers in order.

'Guess what's in here?' She sounded unusually breathless. 'I'll give you one clue. Once you see it you're going to be begging for copies. Go on, guess!'

'Um, the recipe for eternal life?' Ella suggested.

'Pooh,' Nat said sulkily. 'Now it's going to seem like a real let-down.'

'Just teasing,' Ella said, grinning. 'Come on! Put us out of our misery.'

Nat slid out a photograph and gave us a brief tantalising glimpse before she whisked it back out of sight.

'Oh my God, you stole a photograph of Mr Berolli off the board!' breathed Ella.

'I didn't steal it, I *borrowed* it,' Nat corrected primly. 'I'll take it home and scan it into my laptop. Then first chance I get, I'll put it back in the display.' She gave us an anxious little smile. 'We can all have copies to put under our pillows.

I thought you'd be really pleased.'

Ella and I both hugged her.

'You're nuts,' I told her. 'Funny, sweet and *totally* nuts!'

'Want to see what else I borrowed?' she asked casually.

I felt a familiar sinking feeling. 'What?'

'Tada!' Nat slid out a second photo.

Ella and I stared in bewilderment at Miss Simpson's small, bland, completely forgettable face.

'Why would you want to borrow that?' I asked.

Nat gave a little toss of her head, something I had never previously seen her do. 'I told you, a picture is worth a thousand words!'

'Nat,' I said. 'What are you planning?'

'I don't know why you are being so goody-two-shoes all of a sudden, Billie Gold,' Nat said defensively. 'We agreed this is war, remember?'

'Yes, and I asked what are you planning?' I insisted.

Nat slid the photo back into her wallet. 'You'll have to wait and see, won't you?' she told me with a smirk and walked away.

'Would the real Natalie Bonneville-St John please come back?' I said, not quite under my breath.

Ella shook her head. 'Everything's weird since we lost Mario's.'

She didn't add, *Including you, Billie*. But I knew it was what she meant.

I went straight from school to Mr Kaminski's and collected little Bullet. We had a heart-stopping moment with a police car, only I was ready this time and hung on to his lead like grim death.

When we got back, Mr Kaminski asked me if I could replace the light bulb in his reading lamp. I replaced the bulb. Then he asked, very sweetly and apologetically, if I could fetch him a blanket as he was feeling chilly. I fetched the blanket and made him a hot cup of tea. I knew that what he really wanted was someone to talk to. I felt mean but I couldn't be that kind chatty Billie, not today.

On my way out I had to pass Mr Kaminski's dining room. Now that he ate all his meals in front of the TV, the room had become a dumping ground for old furniture. My heart suddenly skipped a beat. On top of a knobbly looking sideboard was an old Aiwa stereo.

I went in and checked. Bingo! It had a tape deck! I ran back into Mr Kaminski. 'Mr Kaminski, I'm sorry to disturb you, but could I try out an old tape in your stereo just to see if it still works?'

He blinked at me through his pebble glasses. He'd been watching *Come Dine with Me*. 'Of course, Billie, any time.'

'Could I run and fetch it now?'

'Whenever you like!' he beamed.

I flew home. 'I'm taking some custard creams for Mr Kaminski,' I called to my mum. 'I've made him a cup of tea and he fancied something sweet.'

My mum sounded touched. 'That's fine, Billie,' she called back from the living room.

Like my mum, I'm usually honest. Maybe honest people make more convincing fibbers because she obviously didn't suspect a thing. I didn't even feel guilty; it was almost scary. Some man in a trilby hat had made a throwaway remark and suddenly I was seeing my mum as a total stranger.

I rushed back to Mr Kaminski's, made him a fresh cup of tea and arranged some of the custard creams on a plate because then it wasn't like I'd told a total lie.

Then I took the cassette into Mr Kaminski's cold, stale-smelling dining room and slipped it into the machine. I pressed PLAY. Eventually it dawned on me that the stereo was turned off at the mains. I switched the power on, pressed PLAY again, leaned against the wall and closed my eyes.

I hadn't admitted this to myself, but I was waiting for the sax solo to end all sax solos: Jimmie Logan, the undiscovered genius, the man who could have topped Gerry Rafferty's *Baker Street* if he'd only got a lucky break.

It wasn't a sax; that was the first surprise. It was a woman singing a song by Joan Armatrading, a song I've always loved, called *Willow*. The singer on the tape had a good voice, bluesy and warm, and naggingly familiar in a way I couldn't quite place.

I angrily clicked off the machine. It wasn't my dad, that's all I cared about. I had let myself believe in a dumb stupid fantasy. I felt so humiliated you'd think someone had been watching.

I grabbed the cassette, and popped back to say goodbye to Mr Kaminski. 'It still works, thank you so much, Mr Kaminski.' My voice sounded fake, as if it belonged to someone else. Back home, I mumbled something about homework and shut myself in my room.

I don't know how long I'd been staring into space when my mobile went.

'What happened to *you*?' Jools asked plaintively. 'I

waited for ages but you didn't come.'

My head flew into focus. 'Oh my God, Jools, I am SO sorry! It totally slipped my mind. I don't know what's wrong with me this week.'

'Hey, no biggie. Just so long as we hook up really soon. What about Saturday afternoon?'

'I'll be there,' I promised. 'And Jools – I do think it's amazing of you to do this benefit, you know, in the circumstances.'

'It's not amazing at all. Freya's mum is my best friend, remember,' Jools said briskly. 'Anyway, life goes on, you know?'

After Jools rang off I sat on my bed doing some hard thinking. Jools' family had lost their home and their business. Yet Jools still had room in her life for other people's problems as well as her own.

Life goes on, you know. She'd said it as if it was just the most normal thing, whereas I'd been feeling like all the world's clocks had stopped for ever. They'd stopped the moment Blues Hat told me, 'Your mother made the right choice.'

Talking to Jools had jolted me out of my self-pity. The cassette had just been a red herring; a random recording my mum had hung on to for no reason, the way she'd hung on to that miniature pack of cards from the Christmas cracker. The man in the hat was just a random contact from my dad's dim distant past. In the end, it came back to one thing. My mum was not a liar. My dad was dead. End of.

That night, I slept so soundly I didn't even wrinkle my sheet. This makes it all the more weird that my deep dreamless sleep came with a haunting soundtrack; a woman's voice half-singing, half-whispering Joan Armatrading's *Willow*.

Chapter Nine

Thursday disappeared in a bit of a blur. My little brother became really poorly overnight so Mum took him to A&E. When he eventually got in to see a doctor, he was diagnosed with viral pneumonia and sent home with antibiotics. Unfortunately, both Mum and Mitch had afternoon meetings they couldn't really cancel. I asked Mrs Salazar if she'd walk Bullet and dashed straight home from school to take charge.

I spent the rest of the afternoon reading dinosaur stories and fetching cooling drinks for my cranky little brother. I felt huge respect for Lexie who looked after her three brothers on a regular basis and hadn't complained once.

My friends sent me jokey texts to try to cheer me up. Like me, they were counting down to the weekend when we could start the hunt for our new café.

Over our packed lunches next day, Nat, Ella and I managed to come up with a shortlist of the cafés we'd be auditioning on Saturday: Café Quirk, the Hub and the Blue Sky Café.

'I can't wait.' Nat said excitedly. 'I can't believe we've only missed one week of the Breakfast Club. It feels more like a decade.'

Maybe it was the prospect of getting back into our Breakfast Club groove that made Nat seem more like her usual lovely self. She'd told us she had scanned in Mr Berolli's photograph and sneaked the photos back into the display without being seen. She said she was waiting 'til we were all together before she gave us our copies because that way it would be more special.

Nat still hadn't explained why she'd wanted Miss Simpson's picture. I hoped that if she'd ever had any real thoughts of revenge, she'd finally come to her senses and decided against them.

'We are going to have so much to talk about this Saturday,' Ella said.

'Why don't we make it an all-day breakfast?' suggested Nat hopefully.

I shook my head. 'I'm meeting Jools later. She asked if I'd—'

Ella quickly held up her hand. 'Don't tell us now!

We're saving all our hot news for tomorrow, remember? Breakfast Club rules!'

Ella was right. My news would keep. 'So which place are we auditioning first?' I asked.

'The Blue Sky Café,' Ella said at once. 'And before you say, that's not just because it's round the corner from me. I just think it sounds really – you know – *uplifting*!'

'Well it *is* a converted church,' I joked.

'Plus my dad is always on about something called "Blue Sky thinking",' Ella explained. 'That's like being really super-positive, isn't it? Instead of always thinking of the worst case scenario? And everyone in the Breakfast Club is a total Blue Sky thinker, or we wouldn't be in it.' she said beaming.

'That's true,' I agreed.

Nat nodded. 'I vote for Blue Sky too.'

'I guess we'd better text Lexie and tell her we're meeting up at the Blue Sky Café then!' I told them happily.

Next morning, I woke to find the words to *Willow* running through my head again as if I'd been listening to the cassette in my sleep. Then I remembered what day it was, and everything else went out of my head as my mind zoomed back to the day we'd invented the Breakfast Club. I heard Ella saying: *Imagine all four of us waking up in our separate homes on a grey nothingy London day like today. At first no one feels like getting up, then you remember. Oh my God! It's Saturday!*

Today was a grey nothingy day all right, one of those days when the clouds come crowding down over London like a woolly lid. But I didn't mind about grey skies, because I was a Blue Sky thinker, like Ella said, and I had Somewhere to Be! I jumped out of bed and put on the jeans and top I currently love the most.

I really love that everyone in the Breakfast Club dresses in their own special style. At our first breakfast at Mario's, Ella had insisted that the whole point was to be ourselves, then added quickly, 'Not our ordinary everyday selves; the selves we'd be if we were starring in our own movie. Our superstar celebrity selves!'

We all met up outside the Blue Sky café at 10.30 on the dot and if I say so myself, we looked *smoking*.

Ella was wearing a lacy gypsy top under a fringed waistcoat with a short, flouncey gypsy skirt, leggings and black and white Converse high tops. Nat was wearing a gorgeous vintage tea-dress and a cute little retro cardi that she and Ella had found on Ella's fave vintage stall. Lexie wore her usual skinny jeans and a cropped denim jacket over a T-shirt with a bright green pea pod on the front. Underneath it said: *Give Peas a Chance*. I was wearing my red plaid Akademiks hoodie, jeans and my Converse trainers.

Lexie said I looked like a budding rock star because I'd brought my guitar along. I started to explain that I'd got to run through my songs with Jools later but Ella shushed me again.

'Tell us when we're all sitting down,' she said. 'Now are we all ready?'

'Am I *ready*?' Lexie squeaked. 'I've been on the ice rink since five-thirty. I'm seriously thinking of gnawing off my own arm!'

The builders who had converted the Blue Sky Café had kept the original church door. It was massive with a huge iron ring for a doorknob. Ella needed both hands to turn it.

Still grasping the ring, she suddenly turned round and said in a teachery voice: 'Now, this isn't going to be anything like Mario's, OK? But that doesn't mean it can't be really vibey in its own special way!'

Afterwards I thought she must have had a peek inside.

We all sailed in through the church-style doors then instinctively drew closer together. 'Wow!' everyone said, but very softly because it felt so disturbingly like going into a church. Also the high ceilings did funny things to the sound, so that even a tiny clink of someone's fork against their plate went dinging and donging around the café. I'm not kidding, it was like the chimes of Big Ben.

'Awesome!' breathed Ella.

I wasn't sure that 'awesome' was what I really wanted from a café. The Blue Sky was certainly classy. The customers all seemed to be wealthy, well-dressed couples. Most of them were silently reading the papers while they ate. Possibly they were couples who didn't like each other?

A few eyebrows shot up when we came in but we ignored them and bravely asked for a table for four.

Anyone can go into a café if they have the money; well, that's the theory. But you can tell when you're not wanted, can't you?

The woman who served us could have got the role of that White Witch who makes Narnia always winter. She gave us a scary little smile, demanded to know what we wanted to drink, then left us with four copies of the Blue Sky's breakfast menu.

'Oh,' said Nat forlornly, after a few minutes of anxious searching. 'Don't they do anything without egg?'

I scanned the menu and saw what she meant. If you didn't like egg you were in for a thin time. They had eggs with cream, eggs with smoked salmon, eggs with ham, eggs with spinach (a double whammy for Nat who can't stand either) and a complicated looking Mexican egg dish with chilli peppers called *Huevos Rancheros*.

'They do omelettes,' Ella suggested. 'Oh, sorry Nat, more eggs.'

'There's kedgeree, Nat,' said Lexie encouragingly.

'With rice, haddock and boiled eggs,' Nat said. 'No thanks.'

'Black pudding?' I said helpfully. 'That hasn't got eggs.'

Nat mimed sticking her fingers down her throat.

'It does sound kind of gross,' I said sympathetically.

Nat shuddered. 'Not to mention they make it out of pig's blood.'

'Oh, you *are* joking,' said Ella.

The White Witch had grudgingly brought our lattes. Now she was hovering frostily with her notepad and pencil.

'We've got to order *something*,' Lexie hissed.

'Has anyone seen the prices?' I whispered.

It turned out that no one had.

'Oh. My. God,' said Ella.

There was a moment of pure panic; then Nat said, 'Down the bottom, look! French toast with maple syrup and berries. That's *almost* affordable.'

'Has it got gold dust sprinkled on it?' Lexie looked in disbelief at the price. 'Oh, bums, let's go for it!'

Ella started pulling weird faces.

'What did I do?' asked Lexie.

'"Bums,"' Ella mouthed. 'We're in a *church*?'

We managed to hold out until the Witch had gone off with our order. Then we all collapsed into giggles which made even more eyebrows go up, which set us off even worse.

Wiping the tears from our faces, we were finally ready to settle down for a good Breakfast Club natter.

Of course we had to tell Lexie all about Mr Berolli and Miss Simpson. Lexie was every bit as shocked as we had hoped. Nat produced her plastic wallet and presented us all with our own photographs of Josh Berolli. After we'd finished swooning, Nat told Lexie how she'd 'borrowed' the pics from the drama group display.

'You are outrageous, Natalie Bonneville-St John,' Lexie told her, and Nat did a little bow and said, 'Why thank you, Alexandra Brown!'

Nobody mentioned what had happened in Food Tech. I thought maybe Ella and Nat felt a tiny bit ashamed of what they'd done?

The White Witch was back with our French toast, which she set down in total icy silence. We looked at it in silent disbelief.

After she'd left, Lexie whispered, 'Is this café supposed to be for dollies?'

The portions were so tiny you could have inhaled them.

'Your step-dad did say "moveable feast" not "invisible feast"?' quipped Nat.

Ella blew out her cheeks. 'OK, I vote we eat our dollies' breakfast and get the bill. Then we'll go and find a real breakfast somewhere friendly!'

We were still hungrily mopping up the last teeny dribbles of maple syrup when our witch waitress appeared and started silently clearing our table. We all exchanged astonished looks.

I had suddenly had enough. I quickly stood up, scraping back my chair.

'You probably haven't realised that we are undercover inspectors for a well-known teenage consumer group,' I told the Witch. 'I'm sorry to tell you that the Blue Sky Café just failed in every single category.' I plunked down my money on the table and the others did the same. 'Obviously we will not be recommending you to our readers,' I finished haughtily.

By the time we got outside we were laughing so hard we literally had to hold each other up.

When she'd recovered, Ella fished out her pen. 'How many stars do you give it? The categories are food, prices, music, ambience.'

'No stars,' I said. 'In any category. Anyway, what music?'

'Not even for ambience?' asked Ella.

'It's a lovely building,' I admitted, 'but that doesn't mean it's got ambience. There are funeral parlours with better vibes than that café.'

'I give it minus stars,' said Nat.

'Me too,' said Lexie.

Ella scratched the Blue Sky off the top of her list. 'Which place next?'

'Café Quirk,' I suggested.

We agreed that this name sounded way cooler than the Blue Sky Café. I could just hear myself saying airily, 'Let's pop over to the Quirk,' or 'Meet you at Quirk's in ten!'

Café Quirk was just ten minutes from the Blue Sky.

Inside, first impressions were good, even if it did look a bit like a spaceship with gleaming chrome fittings everywhere. They had some kind of bubblegum pop music on a loop but at least it was young and fun.

I had just decided that the café was actually more like a kind of hi-tech skating rink than a spaceship when a waitress in jeans and a good-fitting black T-shirt came gliding up on roller blades. Her hair was cut in one of those choppy little bobs that look so great on girls with good bones. The slogan on her T-shirt said *Café Quirk, the Future of Caffeine* and she had a little name badge that said *Tabitha Chan.*

'Hi! Welcome to Café Quirk!' she beamed. 'My name is Tabitha. Is this your first time here?'

'Oh my God, yes!' gushed Ella. 'Oh my God, this is *so* amazing!'

Tabitha gave us another dazzling smile and went straight into her pitch. 'As you may have heard, Café Quirk specializes in quirky and unusual beverages. Over there we have a board showing all the available options. I'll leave you by yourselves for a few moments while you make up your minds, but if you have any queries, just holler, OK?' And Tabitha glided away to welcome some new customers.

We scanned the menu board with growing

excitement. As well as the usual espressos, lattes, cappuccinos and macchiatos, you could have Peppermint Twist (hot milk, peppermint syrup, whipped cream and mint chips), Mint Chocolate Chip Whip (coffee, mint-flavoured hot cocoa, topped with whipped cream and chocolate chip shavings) or a White Chocolate Whip, similar to the Mint Whip, but made with coffee and white chocolate instead of milk chocolate, and instead of mint you had cinnamon sprinkles as well as chocolate chips on your cream topping.

I fancied the one that combined a shot of espresso with chocolate *and* orange syrup, plus grated orange or lemon peel, topped with cream. But there were literally dozens of amazing drinks to choose from.

'If we become regulars, do you think they'd name a drink after us?' Ella asked hopefully.

'It's so young and vibey.' Nat was dreamily watching the waiters swoosh around the floor with trays of tall glasses filled with frothy caffeinated drinks.

'And friendly,' said Lexie. 'Friendly is good.'

'And fun,' said Ella. 'And the music isn't *so* bad.'

It would be fabulous fun to waitress at Café Quirk, I thought. But we were customers and something was missing. 'Don't they serve any food with their exciting beverages?' I asked.

Ella flew off to find Tabitha. 'They have a wide selection of Danish pastries,' she reported back, 'and they also sell high-energy cookies.'

'Where are the tables?' asked Nat.

We had been so distracted by the roller blades and the fun drinks that we hadn't noticed the lack of tables and chairs. It turned out that Café Quirk was too far into the future to have tables. Instead they had space-age counters shaped like extra-long figures of eight, made out of shiny white plastic. Nat said they looked like infinity symbols. To sit at them you had to hoist yourself on to a high stool, also shiny and white.

We sat at a counter, balancing on our stools, and Tabitha brought our drinks and a plate of pastries. The drinks were delicious, though fiercely high in caffeine. The pastries were *meh*.

Bravely chewing our sawdust pastries, trying to stop our elbows sliding off the counters, we told each other that we had never expected to find our perfect café first off.

'I did think we might find some breakfast though,' said Lexie plaintively and we burst out laughing. Fortunately nobody minds you laughing at Café Quirk.

'Oh my God, Lexie!' I remembered. 'First we forgot

your birthday, and now we didn't even ask how you got on in your skating test?'

'That's OK,' she beamed. 'I got on quite well, actually.'

'And?' prompted Ella. 'Come on, Lexie. This is the Breakfast Club. We *celebrate* our achievements. We need details, girl!'

'OK,' said Lexie shyly. 'Well, um, I'm through to Level Eight.'

'Woo-hoo!' everyone cheered. 'Go Lexie!'

'What does that mean?' asked Nat. 'Level Eight?'

'It means I can qualify for the British skating championships,' Lexie explained.

'Wow,' said Nat amazed. 'Well done you!'

'OK, so you've told me the goss about Mr Bertolli,' Lexie said, quickly taking the spotlight off herself. 'What else is new?'

This wasn't our café. Deep down, we had known this from the start. But Mitch was so right about us being a movable feast, because as the conversation zoomed from topic to topic I could feel that old Breakfast Club magic in the air. We were together again and that's all that mattered.

'Oh, Billie,' Ella said excitedly. 'I forgot to say Dad and Naomi got Kitty's parcel. They sent me a pic, look.'

Ella scrolled through the pictures on her phone, and showed us a picture of little Kitty wearing a black and red striped T-shirt dress with a border of tiny skulls over black tights, and the miniature Nikes! To disguise her bald little head they'd put her in a cute headband with a floppy black flower.

'Oh, she's so cuuuute,' said Nat. 'And I don't even *like* babies!'

'That's a great look,' I grinned. 'I just love those skulls!'

'Naomi disapproves of babies wearing pastels,' Ella explained; then her face did a funny little quiver.

'Oh, Ella, what's wrong?' Lexie asked anxiously.

'Annie hasn't seen this photo, has she?' I said.

Ella's eyes were suddenly shiny with tears. 'No, and she mustn't see it either, which means I've got to delete it, and I don't want to have to delete it. If we were a normal family I could have it as my screen saver, you know? I wouldn't have to sneak about.'

'If your mum saw this pic, would she seriously go up the wall?' asked Nat.

'Totally,' said Ella.

'That's rubbish,' said Lexie fiercely. 'Your mum is putting you in a really horrible position and I think—' She quickly checked herself. 'I'm sorry, Ella, it's your mum, you'd probably rather I didn't say?'

'It's OK,' said Ella bravely. 'I can take it.'

Lexie took a deep breath. 'I think she's being a jealous selfish cow, and you shouldn't let her get away with it.'

Nat and I nodded vigorously.

'So you don't think I should delete it?' said Ella.

'No *way*,' said Lexie. 'It's blackmail, Ella! She's trying to make you behave as if Kitty doesn't exist, and that's just mad!'

Ella blinked. 'Oh, thanks! I mean, not for saying my mum's mad, but you know, thanks! I guess I should start standing up to her more?'

Nat drained the last of her Mint Chocolate Chip Whip, then covered her mouth to hide a tiny burp. 'I'm not sure if I'm ready for the caffeine of the future,' she sighed.

'Me neither,' Ella said.

Lexie just managed to save herself from falling off her stool. 'Is anyone else really hungry? Because if I don't get something to mop up some of this caffeine really soon, I'm going to have the screaming hooly-hoos!'

We paid our bill, leaving a small tip for our roller-skating waitress. Lexie said the reason Tabitha was so bubbly and cheerful was probably because she got so many free caffeine drinks as part of her perks.

Outside Café Quirk, Ella said, 'Right, how many stars?'

'It was fun,' I said. 'I give it four stars.'

'Too uncomfortable and the food was grim,' said Nat. 'Three stars.'

'I give it two,' said Lexie. 'I'm marking them down for health and safety.'

We all goggled at her. 'Huh?'

'Those stupid slippery seats,' she explained with a grin. 'Actually, the real reason I marked them down is because too much caffeine, plus a lack of decent food, makes me *really* grumpy.'

Ella gave Café Quirk four stars because of the spaceship decor, bubbly Tabitha and the roller blades.

The last café on our list was the Hub.

'OK, brave hearts, let's go!' said Lexie. 'I don't want to hex it but I have a funny feeling this will be The One.'

'The Hub is such a great name. That's like the place where it all happens,' said Nat dreamily.

'The Happening Place,' Ella giggled. 'That is *definitely* the place for us.'

'Remember when we were little kids? You'd write your address, like, Billie Gold, Ladbroke Grove,

London, the World, the Universe,' I said. 'That's what the Hub makes me think of, like it's the centre of the Universe.'

And linking arms, our veins zinging with caffeine, we swept off to the Hub for Part Three of our great Café Quest.

Chapter Ten

We pushed open the door to our third and final café of the day.

'Oh, this is – *different*,' said Nat in her polite boarding-school voice.

'Very different,' I agreed.

New Age music tinkled on the sound system like annoying little wind chimes. The chairs and tables were hewn from what looked like chunks of naked tree. On the walls were pictures of gnarled old peasants holding vegetables that they had obviously just dug out of the earth with their arthritic old hands.

'So, um, how did you get to hear about this café, Lexie?' asked Nat.

'My parents,' Lexie said bitterly. 'I should have known.'

'Oh, I get it now,' breathed Ella. 'It's an *eco* café!'

'It's a *hippie* café,' said Lexie through stiff lips. 'I can smell hippie food.'

Nat cautiously sniffed the air. 'I don't think I know what hippie food actually smells like.'

'It just smells like a regular café to me,' I said.

'OK, maybe we can't smell it yet, but they'll have hippie food on the menu, trust me,' Lexie said.

'You can't know that for sure,' Nat objected.

'I can smell lentils a mile away,' snapped Lexie.

Ella tutted. 'Come on, Lexie, it's our last café. Give it a chance.'

She looked despairing. '*Must* we?'

'Movable feast, remember?' I reminded her. 'We can be the Breakfast Club anywhere: in a church, a skating rink . . .'

We were still hovering by the door while we decided what to do.

'OK,' Lexie sighed. 'Let's have the full hippie breakfast before I die of malnutrition.'

A young guy wearing a Hub T-shirt and faded jeans had been tactfully keeping busy in the background while we had our whispered consultation. I caught his eye, not sure if we had to be told where to sit. He flashed us a sweet smile. 'I'll be over in a sec. Just find a free table and sit down.'

'That shouldn't be hard,' whispered Nat, looking around the almost empty café. I could see Lexie secretly checking out the waiter. So were me and Ella. Young, tall, soft dark curls. We exchanged smirks. Things were looking up!

We arranged ourselves around a circular slab of tree. 'Does anyone else feel like a hobbit in *The Lord of the Rings*?' Nat asked in a whisper.

To our surprise, the Hub had loads better breakfast choices than the Blue Sky. You could have porridge with maple syrup and cream. You could have stacks of pancakes with berries and different fillings. You could have waffles, bacon, beans, mushrooms, hash browns – and the prices weren't bad either.

The curly-headed guy finally made his leisurely way over to our table. 'Hi, I'm Daniel and as you see I'm the only waiter in sight!' he joked. 'What can I get you ladies?'

Even Ella was completely caffeined-out, so we all ordered organic fruit smoothies. When our food came the portions were proper portions, not doll-sized. We took cautious mouthfuls, in case a few stray lentils had got secretly smuggled into our hash browns.

Our waiter, Daniel, watched with an amused expression. 'Everything OK, ladies?' He had a faint accent that was either Aussie or New Zealand.

'Way better than OK,' Ella told him, beaming with relief. 'Really yummy!'

'Someone told us this was a hippie café so we weren't sure what the food would be like,' Nat explained.

'*Natalie!*' hissed Ella.

Luckily Daniel didn't seem offended. 'Easy mistake to make,' he grinned.

'Why is it so empty when the food's so great?' asked Ella.

'Our main business is organic catering,' he explained. 'I think the owners are letting the café side of things run down. It probably won't be here much longer.'

We had never seriously thought this was going to be our café, but now we knew for sure we would have to keep on looking. Everybody looked just a little bit down in the dumps.

Daniel was just strolling back to his post by the cash desk when Lexie called, 'Excuse me, but do we have to listen to that music?'

He looked surprised. 'Is it getting on your nerves?'

'Isn't it getting on yours?' asked Lexie.

'It did, when I first started,' he admitted. 'I don't actually notice it now. I'll go and turn it down.'

Lexie had a crooked grin on her face like her little brother Clem gets when he's about to say something really cheeky. 'I've got a better idea,' she said. 'Our friend Billie here mixed me a CD for my birthday. Could we play it on your sound system? If you get busy, you could take it off.'

Daniel hesitated, then said, 'Sure, why not?'

Lexie gave him the CD and he went over to slot it into the machine.

'Lexie Brown, you are outrageous!' I hissed.

'Hey, if you don't ask, you don't get,' she said cheerfully.

I was watching Daniel's face when the CD started to play, so I saw him trying to hide his disappointment as The Skaters' Waltz came out of the speakers, then his look of pleased surprise as it almost instantly morphed into thumping hip hop. 'Nice!' he grinned, holding up his thumb.

'Billie's a good DJ,' Lexie told him.

'She's a good DJ but she's a brilliant singer-songwriter,' Ella said loyally.

It was a kind of dreamlike feeling sitting in a public café listening to music that I had put together in the privacy of my bedroom. When I heard my voice come on chatting over the music, I suddenly felt like I wanted to hide; then all these other emotions came welling up out of nowhere.

'Billie, are you OK?' Ella asked anxiously.

Nat patted my hand. 'If you've got a worry, you have to share it. Breakfast Club rules.'

I'd got so many worries lately they were stacking up like planes over Heathrow; but they were personal, painful worries that I didn't feel able to share with anyone, and certainly not in a public place. But seeing my friends quietly waiting, I thought it couldn't hurt to share my latest smallest worry.

'I promised Jools I'd sing at a fundraiser they're holding for her friend's little girl,' I explained. 'It's a really good cause, plus it would be my first ever professional gig.'

Ella gasped. 'Oh my God, Billie, that is *so* brilliant. You must be thrilled!'

Was I thrilled? I'd had so much going on in my life lately that I hadn't had a free moment to think how I actually felt.

'I am,' I confessed. 'Well, I was when Jools initially asked me. But when Mario's closed down I assumed they'd just drop the whole idea. I guess I didn't really know Jools.'

'She really is quite a girl,' said Lexie admiringly.

'So what's the problem, Billie?' asked Nat.

'I stupidly promised Jools I'd do it, without running it past my mum first,' I told them.

'She's not exactly going to say no, is she?' Lexie objected. 'I mean, firstly it's a brilliant cause, and secondly you finally get to perform your songs in front of an audience. It's like win-win-win!'

I shook my head. 'It's a bit more complicated than that, Lexie. Basically my mum doesn't think being a singer or a musician is a proper grown-up job.'

'Wasn't your dad a musician?' Ella said, perplexed.

'That could be part of the problem,' I said miserably. 'It's hard to know for sure though, since my mum refuses ever to discuss it.'

Lexie set down her smoothie glass with a sharp little clink. 'Well, I'm sorry, but I think your mum is going to have to lighten up on this one.'

'I agree,' said Nat.

'Me too,' said Ella.

'It's like she thinks music is going to like, *destroy* me, and I'm going to end up injecting drugs and living in a squat. It makes me wonder if she even *knows* me, you know?' The bitter words just came bursting out. I was struggling to keep my feelings under control. You let out one small trouble and the others just come galloping through the gap like runaway horses.

'Billie, you are never ever going to end up on drugs,' Nat said firmly.

'Because you're going to be the next Lily Allen!' said Ella.

To my surprise, Lexie reached out and lightly smacked my hand. 'You're always really wise for other people,' she said affectionately, 'but you're rubbish at taking care of yourself.'

I thought this was unfair. 'I am *constantly* taking care of myself, Lexie! Why do you think I do three jobs?'

'Yes, but the Breakfast Club is about living your dream, right? And Billie, music *is* your dream.' Lexie's eyes were suddenly shining.

I felt my eyes fill with tears. 'I know! But just lately, living my dream sometimes feels – *really* hard.' I heard my voice wobble, and turned hastily to Ella to take some of the heat off. 'So what's *your* dream, Ella?'

She went a little bit pink. 'Actually my dream has kind of changed recently,' she said shyly. 'I've decided I want to go to college and train to be a fashion designer.'

'I thought you wanted to be a supermodel!' said Lexie.

'I did, but I've been thinking and I don't think I'd

like being stared at and photographed all the time. What I really love is fashion and I love knowing all the new looks that are coming in.'

We all nodded earnestly. Ella was brilliant at predicting up-and-coming styles and colours. She was already doing it at primary school. It was like a kind of sixth sense.

'I've decided I'd rather have a say in the clothes that models wear than be a model myself,' she confessed. 'I mean, my drawing skills aren't that great yet, but I've got time to improve, right?'

'I think you'd be a brilliant designer, Ella,' I said at once. 'I can just see you at the Clothes Show, all the models strutting down the catwalk wearing your clothes!'

'Plus you're already living in the perfect city,' Nat told her. 'London is the fashion capital of the world, or so my sisters keep telling me,' she added with a sigh.

'I think it's a great idea,' said Lexie. 'When I'm a famous figure skater, you can design all my costumes!'

'And you've got the perfect name for a designer: Ella Swanson,' I said. 'You'd better give us good discounts though, or we'll sell scandalous stories about you to the tabloids.' I sneaked a look at my watch. 'Sorry, guys, but I've got to go. I'm meeting Jools in twenty minutes so we can run through my songs.' I quickly counted out my share of the bill.

'You can't go yet,' Ella objected. 'You haven't said how many stars you rate the Hub.'

'OK, um, grumpy old peasants and gnarly tree-trunks one star. Food and prices four stars each.' I slid my eyes mischievously in the direction of the cute waiter. 'Service five stars!' I added in a whisper. 'Original background music, um . . . ten stars!'

Everyone laughed and Lexie said loyally, 'Definitely ten stars for the music! Where are you meeting Jools, anyway?'

'At the Grove.'

Ella's eyes went wide. 'Freya's fund-raiser is going to be at the Grove? Wow, Billie, how starry are you?'

Just at that moment, I did feel genuinely starry. With my music playing and my friends smiling encouragement, it suddenly felt really good to be me.

'Next week we'll nail it, Ella,' I told her confidently. 'We'll find our café. I know we will.'

'Hey, it'll happen!' she beamed.

'What are you going to do when you get back home?' I asked Nat.

'Me?' Nat said carelessly. 'Oh, I thought I'd have a little play with Photoshop.'

'I never knew you could use Photoshop,' said Ella in surprise.

'I couldn't, I asked Oliver to teach me.'

Nat suddenly sounded edgy. I had a feeling something was off, but I didn't have time to worry about her now so I just said, 'Well, have fun!'

'I'm going home to have a hot bath, then I'm going to put my PJs on and my earplugs in and have a lovely long sleep,' said Lexie, yawning.

'Later, OK?' I blew them all kisses, and slinging my guitar over my shoulder, I set off to the Grove.

Chapter Eleven

Our marathon Breakfast Club session had given my confidence a much-needed boost, but when I eventually emerged from the Grove, I was totally buzzing!

We'd discussed my set. Jools was visibly relieved when I said I'd be bringing my own backing CD as well as accompanying myself on my acoustic guitar. She'd been worried I'd demand some super-technical set-up.

Jools' boyfriend was there for the whole meeting. His name is Louis and he's a really cool guy. We used to see him all the time at Mario's. Louis is a professional events organiser and he'd been helping Jools to make her fundraiser happen.

There were two other guys with Jools that I vaguely remembered seeing at Mario's. One was the sound engineer; the other guy, Larry, was the actual owner of the Grove, and there were some other people from the Grove as well. At first I felt a bit overwhelmed, thinking of all the famous artists who'd performed on the stage where we were standing. But Jools, Louis and the others were lovely, making me feel that I had a right to be there.

I quickly went through my songs and when I finished, Larry did this slow pleased smile, as if I'd really surprised him. Everyone else cheered and clapped, and the sound man said, 'Woo-hoo! I'm going to tell Lily she'd better look out!'

I almost had a heart attack when Jools told me the benefit was next Friday. That was less than a week away! 'Boy, I'd better do some serious rehearsing between now and then!' I said anxiously.

'Just sing like you did just now and everyone will love you, Billie,' Jools said, and I felt a tiny *zing* inside my heart that told me she really meant it.

On the way home I was practically flying. I felt as if I'd crossed a major bridge into my future life as a singer-songwriter. By the time I went in through our front door, I wasn't a fourteen-year-old girl who had to ask her mum's permission to perform. I was Billie Gold, Jimmie Logan's daughter. I was my superstar celebrity self.

I found Mitch and Finlay on the sitting-room floor trying to do a huge jigsaw puzzle. It wasn't a particularly hard puzzle, but Sparkle was complicating things as usual by batting the crucial pieces away with her paw.

'We told her she could have the pieces of sky,' Finlay explained earnestly. 'But she only wants the dinosaurs.' He was still pale and he wasn't putting out the normal Finlay-type decibels, but his little gap-toothed grin showed that he was on the mend.

'Where's Mum?' I asked Mitch. 'I've got something to tell her.'

He gave a surprised laugh. 'You sound very business-like all of a sudden! I think she's catching up on some washing and ironing.'

There's a lean-to conservatory off our kitchen which we've adapted as a utility room and general dumping ground. Mum was in there with the washer and the drier going full blast. The room smelled of hot soap and clean ironing. She looked up from ironing one of the print blouses she wears for work. 'Hi, you! Did you find your perfect café?'

'Not yet.' I took a deep breath. 'Mum, I've just been to the Grove and I thought you should know that I'm performing there on Friday night.'

My mum gasped as if I'd hit her. 'You – you were at a *club*?'

'Yes, and I went through my set and they thought it was fine and—'

Mum put the steam iron down so fast that a jet of scalding water came spurting out. 'Slow down, Billie,' she said, and I could tell she was fighting to keep her cool. 'Let me get my head around this. You went to a club and you auditioned—'

'It wasn't an audition,' I said, impatient at having to explain. 'It was just to give them an idea of what I can do. But they totally loved my stuff, even Larry, he's like the owner of the Grove, and I'm going to be doing a proper set, so it's actually a brilliant—'

I had never heard my mother sound so angry. 'No, Billie! You are a fourteen-year-old child. There is no way I am letting you do a *gig* in a *club*.' She made the words sound like something you'd wipe off your shoe.

If my mum was mad, I was absolutely livid. 'I am not a child, Mum, and I am *doing* it, OK? They're expecting me to be there and I'm not letting them down just because you have this weird—'

'Letting them down!' my mum thundered. 'What about letting *me* down? We made an *agreement*, Billie, that you could do your music so long as it didn't interfere with your school work. We agreed that you would just treat it like a *hobby*! Doing late-night gigs at the Grove is not part of that agreement, so you can go and phone Harry or whatever his name is right now, and tell him you're sorry but you will not be performing at his club on Friday night.'

'A *hobby*?' I shrieked. 'What kind of lame stupid word is that? Collecting Motown records is a hobby. Making music is my LIFE, Mum!'

'What's going on, Nina?' Mitch was standing in the doorway, looking bewildered.

'Stay out of it, Mitch,' snapped Mum. 'I'm handling it, thank you.'

This comment totally tipped me over the edge. I filled my lungs with air and I screamed right in her face. 'You are not "handling" anything! You are not my social worker, Mum, and I don't care about your freaking agreement! I am going to sing at the Grove on Friday night and you can't stop me!'

I stormed off to my room. Behind me I heard Mitch saying, 'What was that about singing at the Grove?'

'Mitch, I told you to stay out of it!' Mum yelled.

'No, I *won't* stay out of it!' Mitch yelled back. 'This is my family too and I need to know what the HELL is going on!'

In all the time he had lived with us, I had never known Mitch to raise his voice. As I slammed my door I heard my brother burst into scared wails.

'Why is everybody shouting? I don't like it when people shout!'

I spent the rest of the day locked in my room. At first I was full of cold rage. I said to myself over and over, 'I hate her, I HATE her.' I kicked my bed (Ow!). I threw stuff. I screamed into my pillow. It just made me feel even more stupid and helpless.

After my anger faded I was left feeling exhausted and depressed. I'd told my mum she couldn't stop me but the truth was, she could. I was fourteen. I was totally dependent on her and Mitch. Everything I owned I had because they'd given it to me: my clothes, my guitar, my phone, my laptop. She had all the power and I had none, nada, zero.

Mitch came to try and persuade me to come out. 'Billie, please, we need to talk about this.'

No, actually, we don't, I thought. When adults tell you they need to talk to you about something, what they really mean is, 'We're going to force you to see our point of view.' But that wasn't going to happen. I'd made up my mind that I was never talking to my mum ever again. OK, she may have had all the power, but I had my pride.

I don't know how angry teenagers coped in olden times. I might have been a virtual prisoner in my room but at least I had my phone. I spent the first part of the evening texting my friends, telling them what a cruel evil cow my mum was being. I had never ever used language like that about my mum.

Ella immediately texted back saying: hav u bin smoking drugz?

It took several more texts before I convinced my bewildered friends that this shocking situation with my mum was for real. Then they showered me with comforting messages. Lexie was sure my mum would come round; I just had to give her time. But my friends only knew half the story. I hadn't told them about the cassette or the stranger at Portobello Market. I hadn't told them I had lost all trust in my mum.

My friends meant well, but their cheery upbeat messages only made me feel even more alone. In the end I turned off my phone, put in my ear-buds, turned up my MP3 player and listened to all my moodiest, most heartbreaking tracks, including Gerry Rafferty's *Baker Street*. But all the sax-playing in the world couldn't drown out the words that were going dizzily around in my head. *Your mother made the right choice. Your mother made the right choice. Your mother . . .*

Blues Hat must have known my mum and dad in the early days of their relationship. They'd met when she was really young, not yet twenty-one. Maybe Mum had felt too young to have a baby? Maybe she'd decided to have me adopted but someone (my dad?) had persuaded her to change her mind. Perhaps Blues Hat had meant my mum did the right thing by keeping me because I had turned out OK after all.

I took out my ear-buds. That had to be it. Mum had never wanted me in the first place. That's why she was punishing me like this. I'd ruined her life and now she was ruining mine because deep down she wished I'd never been born.

I told myself I didn't care. I was fourteen, practically grown up. I didn't need a mother. I didn't need anyone. Like my dad, I would live only for my music from now on. Unlike people, music never lets you down.

I had reached a decision. No matter what my mum threatened, I was determined to keep my promise. I was going to sing at little Freya Harrison's fundraiser. If Mum couldn't live with that, it was simple: I would run away from home.

* * *

On Sunday morning I came out of my room to use the bathroom. Then I took a deep breath and went into the kitchen where I silently helped myself to cereal. Mum and I mutually ignored each other.

Before this weekend, we had never stopped talking for even half an hour. We'd been friends as well as mother and daughter. I'd heard my friends going on about how they hated their mothers and I'd felt sorry for them, but I couldn't actually imagine how that could ever happen. Now I knew.

Mitch tried to coax me to stay in the kitchen and have some pancakes but I wouldn't even look at him. As far as I was concerned I'd already left home. I'd do the concert, pack my bag with a few essentials, grab my guitar and leave. It's not like anyone would really care. My dad was the only person who'd ever really loved me and he was long dead. Finlay might miss me for a while, but he was only five; he'd soon forget.

That evening I waited until Mum was in the bathroom helping Finlay wash his hair. Then I went into the kitchen and microwaved myself a baked potato, dumped it on a plate with half a small tub of coleslaw and carried my meal back to my room.

'All the major food groups I see,' Mitch said humorously as I bumped into him in the corridor. I brushed past him without a word, slamming my door in his face.

Monday came and I forced myself to go to school. My friends tried to get me to tell them what had been going on but I refused to talk about it. In my head I had gone from being a normal person with friends and a family to being a homeless girl wandering the streets, alone except for her guitar.

There was only one thought that was stopping me from falling to pieces. On Friday, come hell or high water, I was going to sing at the Grove.

Tuesday and Wednesday came and went.

Midway through Thursday afternoon, a hideous electronic buzzing started up. Everybody groaned. We hadn't had a fire drill in ages. Our history teacher, Miss Tempest, looked a bit surprised, then told us we had to leave the school premises calmly and quietly and wait outside in the playground with all the other classes.

Outside a cold drizzle was coming down, the kind of rain that's so fine it's almost like mist. We all stood there, damp and shivering, waiting for the teachers to start taking the registers, longing to go back inside in the dry and warm.

I heard Miss Simpson and Josh Berolli talking in lowered voices.

'I never received a message about a fire drill or I wouldn't have told my class to put their shepherd's pies in the ovens,' Miss Simpson complained.

'I didn't get a message either,' said Mr Berolli. 'Someone must have slipped up.'

There was a familiar earsplitting wail and three fire engines raced into the playground. People cheered as the firefighters jumped out of their vehicles and started dragging out their equipment.

'Three fire engines, wow,' someone said, impressed. 'They don't usually send fire engines.'

'Is this a fire drill or a terrorist attack, sir?' someone asked Mr Berolli, only half joking.

'My sister was almost in that bus that blew up, you know,' Alice Hussey announced to anybody who might be listening.

'Your sister would be,' Fareeda said under her breath.

'I think there might actually be a fire,' Mr Bertolli said to Miss Simpson. 'There's a strong smell of burning coming from somewhere.'

'The science block, sir!' someone said urgently.

For the first time I saw smoke and flames coming from the chemistry lab.

Ella was too interested in the possible chemistry between Miss Simpson and Josh Berolli to notice. 'She's *really* into him, it's so sad,' she hissed. 'Because I honestly don't think he's remotely into her.'

I glanced around. 'Where's Nat?' I said sharply. 'Didn't she come out with us?'

'I think she just dashed back for something. Do you think he's just better at hiding his feelings?' Ella asked, sounding more anxious about Mr Berolli than Nat. 'My mum says men are so much better at hiding their emotions.'

I was mentally replaying our exit from the classroom and this time I remembered how Nat had made an excuse and ducked into the girls' toilets. *She's just been waiting for an opportunity to pull some little stunt*, I thought. The minute the fire alarm went she'd seized her chance.

Then I thought, *Oh my God! She doesn't know it's a real fire!*

I went flying back across the playground and almost smacked right into Nat.

'Where's the fire?' she said without thinking, then gave a shriek of laughter. 'That was funny!'

'The fire is in the chemistry lab, you mad cow!' I hissed. 'I was coming to find you because I saw smoke and flames and I didn't know where the hell you were!'

Nat's eyes went wide. 'Oh, *Billie*! You were coming to rescue me! That is so incredibly brave!'

She tried to throw her arms around me but I pushed her off. She had given me a bad fright and I was hopping mad.

'What were you up to in there?' I demanded.

'Nothing,' she said at once.

'You're a terrible liar,' I told her. 'I know you were up to something so don't even bother denying it.'

Nat did her huffy face. 'No need to go all Gestapo on me. I just *modified* Miss Simpson's picture a bit, that's all. It's just a joke. God, Billie, lighten up!'

I was disgusted with her. 'Does Oliver know that's why you wanted him to teach you to use Photoshop? So you could do something incredibly dumb with Miss Simpson's photo?'

'Of course he doesn't, and for your information I did not do something incredibly dumb! You haven't even seen what I did to it. It's actually *hilarious*, and it's not my fault you're having a major sense of humour failure.'

'And when Oliver finds out what you did, will he think it's *hilarious* too?'

Mrs Gildersleeve suddenly appeared beside us. 'What do you girls think you are doing?' she fumed. 'You do realise there's a fire? Will you please stay in your designated groups. Your teachers are *trying* to take the register!'

They kept us standing outside for ages. At last the fire engines drove away and the head came out and announced that it was safe to return to our classes.

As I followed Ella into school I could feel this, like, *ripple* of scandal spreading through the foyer. A group of girls including the Alphas were goggling at the school drama society's display.

'Oh my God! It's hilarious!'

'What do you mean, Pia? It's her spitting image!' That was Tamsin.

'I'd love to see her expression when she sees it!'

'She's going to want to crawl away and *die*!' That was Alice Hussey.

'That will teach her to tell me to beat stupid egg whites!' said Pia.

I only had a few seconds. Any time now Miss Simpson would be coming in and the poo would totally hit the fan.

I quickly elbowed my way to the front and saw that Nat had 'modified' Miss Simpson by giving her a friendly green cartoon face.

'I am always going to be calling her Shrek from today,' Isabella announced.

'Or "Troll Face"?' suggested Alice Hussey with a snigger.

Nat was eagerly watching the Alphas. For a few seconds she seemed to be lapping up their reaction. Then her smile faded and she suddenly looked unsure.

I heard Pia say, 'We should make copies, blow up poster-size, and put all over school!'

'That isn't going to happen,' I said. Reaching over Pia's head, I tore down the picture and ripped it into little pieces.

'Billie Gold, *what* do you think you're doing?'

I almost died of fright. Mr Berolli had been standing right behind me!

Before I could say anything, Nat leapt to my defence. 'It wasn't Billie,' she blurted. 'Mr Berolli, you've got to believe me, she hasn't done anything wrong.'

'Thank you, Natalie,' he said, 'but I just saw Billie rip down a picture from a school display. Now I'm waiting for an explanation.'

'I can't explain, sir, I'm sorry.' I heard my voice wobble and angrily told myself I was not going to lose it in front of the Alphas.

'The rest of you get back to your classes,' Mr Berolli ordered. 'You too Natalie.'

As soon as they'd gone, he silently held out his hand and I dropped the torn pieces into his palm. Mr Berolli barely glanced at them (though I think he clocked the giveaway scraps of slime green) before quickly slipping them into his pocket.

A split second later, Mrs Gildersleeve came bustling up with Miss Simpson to see what was going on. 'Is there a problem, Mr Berolli?' A whiff of trouble to Mrs Gildersleeve is like fabulous French perfume to you and me.

'No, everything's fine!' He gave her a businesslike smile. 'I just need a quiet word with Billie.'

Miss Simpson quickly took the hint and went off to her class. Mrs Gildersleeve went stomping down the corridor looking like a vampire who'd been cheated out of her litre of human blood.

'I'm still waiting for an explanation, Billie,' Mr Berolli said quietly.

'I know what it must have looked like, sir, but I didn't put that picture in the display,' I said miserably. 'I tore it down because I didn't want any more people to see it, sir, especially not Miss Simpson.'

He sighed. 'I really want to believe you, but something

about this feels really fishy.'

'I know, sir. It's it's all a bit complicated, sir.'

Mr Berolli rubbed his hands over his face. I think he'd been having a tiring day. 'Billie, I don't want to pry but we've all noticed that you haven't been your usual sparkling self. Are you having some trouble at home?'

Trouble at *home*? I almost laughed. There was trouble everywhere I looked. Little girls born with cerebral palsy for no reason, lovely people like Mario being forced out of business, Nat going off the rails, this nightmare with my mum. Now on top of everything, Mr Berolli thought I was a really bad, spiteful person.

'Will you have to write to my parents, sir?' I almost whispered.

Next minute I thought how mad it was to be worrying about the school sending a letter to my home. I'd forgotten that this time next week I wouldn't actually *have* a home.

Mr Berolli blew out his breath with a little *pfft* sound and I saw him reach a decision. 'OK, Billie, I'm giving you the benefit of the doubt. I don't know how deeply you were involved in this questionable practical joke, but I believe you genuinely wanted to spare Miss Simpson's feelings. But do yourself a favour, OK? Try to stay out of trouble for the rest of the week.'

I could have cried. Not because he had let me off with a warning, but because he obviously didn't think I was a bad person. I didn't think I could bear it if Mr Berolli thought I was a bad person.

When I returned to my class, I could feel everyone's eyes following me as I made my way back to my seat. They were all trying to figure out what in the world was going on, except Nat and Ella who both looked sick with worry. As I passed them, Nat pushed a crumpled note into my hand. What happened? Are you OK?

'I'm fine,' I whispered, managing a weak smile. 'I didn't tell him anything, don't worry.'

At home time Nat and Ella caught up with me by the classroom door.

They both wore identical nervous but determined expressions, like they were on some kind of shared mission.

'Billie, I'd like you to come back to mine for supper,' Nat said awkwardly. 'Ella's coming, aren't you Ella? We texted Lexie but she's got to rehearse for some skating thing.'

'What's going on?' I asked suspiciously.

I thought I'd caught a fleeting look between my friends, but Nat said quickly, 'Why should something be going on? I got you into trouble and I want to make it up to you, that's all.'

'Please, Billie,' Ella pleaded. 'We've hardly seen you all week. We could walk Bullet with you, then we could go back to Nat's.'

'You'd seriously come with me to walk Bullet?' I was amazed. Ella is not exactly famous for physical activity.

'I said so, didn't I?' she said slightly huffily.

'Won't your step-mum mind?' I asked Nat.

Nat shook her head. 'She won't be there. She's taken my sisters to some big charity gala in the West End. It will just be the three of us – well, and Mrs Nolan, but she always loves it when you guys come. And I could make us all something to eat.'

I hesitated. Then I felt this leaden sensation in the pit of my stomach as I realised I had absolutely nothing to go home for. 'OK,' I told them.

I sent Mitch a text telling him I was going back to Nat's but I wouldn't be late. I didn't want them calling out the police on top of everything else.

All the way to Mr Kaminski's, Nat kept on apologising for how she'd behaved. 'I'm so ashamed, Billie. I've been totally bonkers. I wouldn't blame you if you never spoke to me again.'

'Everyone goes a bit bonkers sometimes,' I said.

'No, honestly, I don't know what got into me. It was like I was obsessed. All I could think about was ways to humiliate Miss Simpson. Then when my plan finally started to work and I saw the Alphas and everyone laughing like hyenas, I suddenly had this horrible feeling, like now I was one of them.' Nat actually shuddered. 'That was a scary wake-up call.'

'Nat, I promise you that if you ever show signs of becoming an Alpha, Ella, Lexie and me will kill you,' I teased her.

'No need,' Ella said, straight-faced. 'Tamsin would have got there first. She's been trying to get in with them forever!'

'Oh, so you are the girls from Billie's famous Breakfast Club!' Mr Kaminski said, beaming when I ushered Nat and Ella into his sitting room. 'Let me see, you must be Ella, and you are Natalie, is that right? You didn't bring Lexie with you, Billie? Oh, perhaps she is at the ice rink today?'

I was amazed and touched. I'd had no idea that Mr Kaminski had been taking in all my random burblings about the girls in the Breakfast Club. He seemed thrilled that I had finally brought some of my friends to meet him.

He brought out the latest photos of his grandkids in Canada and Ella and Nat were politely admiring.

'And we've heard all about *you*, Bullet,' Ella told Mr Kaminski's dog. 'I didn't realise he was so short and stumpy though,' she whispered.

'Shut up!' I told her. 'You'll hurt his feelings. Bullet's my mate, aren't you? My short, stumpy little mate!'

We all went into fits of laughter, including Mr Kaminski even though he had no idea what he was laughing at.

We walked Bullet round the block. Then we made Mr Kaminski a hot cup of tea, found the TV remote (as usual he'd lost it down the side of his armchair), said our goodbyes to him and Bullet and hurried off to catch the bus to Nat's.

'Is he alone in that flat all day every day?' asked Nat as we waited at the bust stop.

'Not all day,' I said. 'There are carers who visit and Mrs Salazar pops in now and then for a chat.' Now I'd said it out loud I felt a genuine pang. For the first time I realised that Mr Kaminski's life was depressingly bleak.

'He's still so interested in everything,' said Ella. 'I can't believe he knew all about us!'

Nat did a little shiver. 'I don't ever want to get old.'

'I do!' said Ella to my surprise. 'I am going to be outrageous but fabulously sexy and elegant, like Helen Mirren!'

We hardly ever go to Nat's, at least not when her step-mum and sisters are there. Even when Jenny and the sisters aren't there, the atmosphere isn't that welcoming, like they've left a kind of toxic residue.

Lucky Jenny's dogs didn't seem to share her prejudice against common state-school kids. They came rushing up to sniff us and say hello. Jenny has two cocker spaniel bitches called Tulip and Rosie, and a cocker spaniel male called Hamish McTavish. Nat said those weren't their official Kennel Club names, just their family names.

'Where are Tulip's puppies?' I asked at once.

'We have to keep them in a cage in the kitchen,' Nat explained. 'Otherwise they poo and wee everywhere.'

The puppies were all speckled black and grey with curly ears that made them look like they were wearing teeny little judges' wigs. As soon as they saw us they dashed up to the wire walls of the cage and started whimpering and squeaking and jumping up.

Of all the rooms in the Bonneville-St Johns' huge high-ceilinged house, I feel most comfortable in their kitchen, possibly because Plum, Nellie and Jenny don't spend much time there. Since Nat's family practically never throws anything away, everything is so retro that it's actually coming back into style. The old-style dresser, the huge refrigerator and the cooker are all ancient and a bit shabby around the edges but were scrubbed and polished by Mrs Nolan to a friendly gleam.

Nat made us her speciality cheese on toast, which sounds a bit worthy but was actually delicious. She said she only dares to make it when Jenny and her sisters are safely out of the way. Apparently her dad invented the recipe when he was up at Oxford. Nat said she was allowed to tell us two of his three secret ingredients, which were strong English mustard and Worcestershire sauce. Her dad had made her promise on the family bible that she would never divulge the third ingredient to a living soul.

'What, not even your own husband?' Ella teased.

'No, my dad was extremely clear about that,' Nat said, straight-faced. 'Only if the poor man was on his deathbed and about to breathe his last, then Dad said that might just be allowable.'

Whenever Nat told us stories about Mr Bonneville-St John, I thought he sounded like such a nice funny dad. It was just a shame he was hardly ever around to keep an eye on his youngest daughter.

While Nat was hunting for ingredients in the huge refrigerator, I'd had a disturbing glimpse into her family's eating habits. There was an entire shelf dedicated to fancy cheeses, sausage and cold meats for Mr Bonneville-St John. The other shelves were empty except for low-calorie ready meals, bottles of mineral water and bags of lemons.

We ate at the kitchen table with the dogs lolling happily at our feet. Mrs Nolan occasionally came in and out, but mostly she tactfully left us by ourselves. From how she talked to Nat you could see that she had a really soft spot for her.

After we'd finished eating, Ella sat back. Though I quickly lowered my eyes, I could feel her thoughtfully studying my face.

'Now tell us what's going on, Billie,' she said quietly. 'Don't tell us you're fine because you are SO not fine.'

I felt every muscle suddenly go tense. I scowled at her. 'I knew it. This is a set-up, isn't it?'

'Totally,' Ella said without a trace of shame. 'Lexie told us we had to get it out of you or she'd send the local bad boys round to sort you out.'

For a moment I thought I was going to cry. My friends might not understand my problems but they really, truly cared.

I was just opening my mouth when Nat said urgently, 'Wait! She has to cuddle Betty!' She ran to the puppies' cage, scooped up the smallest puppy, came back to the table and dropped Betty squirming into my arms. 'OK,' she said solemnly. 'Now you can speak.'

With a madly licky puppy to give me courage, I started to pour out my story. I went right back to the beginning when Mum lied about the music cassette, and explained how everything had started going downhill from then.

'So what did you think was on the cassette?' Ella asked.

'I thought it was a recording of my dad playing his sax. I thought that's why Mum had hung on to it all these years.'

'But it wasn't him?' said Nat.

I shook my head. 'It was just some female singer, probably an old friend of my dad's.'

'But why wouldn't your mum want you to know about the tape?' asked Ella. 'Unless . . .'

'Unless what?'

'Don't get mad, OK? But maybe this mystery woman and your dad, you know—'

I wanted to say, 'No way!' But then I thought maybe that was it. Maybe Dad had an affair. Maybe he didn't just leave like Mum always said. Maybe she had kicked him out.

'Hmm,' said Nat. 'If Billie's dad had an affair with the mystery singer and Billie's mum knew about it, why would she hang on to the cassette? If that was me I'd, like, stamp on it and *smash* it into tiny little pieces or pour petrol over it and set light to it!' She saw our startled faces. 'Wouldn't you?' she said, surprised. 'I *definitely* wouldn't keep it as a permanent reminder.'

Ella nodded agreement. 'That's true actually. Apart from anything else, you wouldn't want your daughter finding it and asking awkward questions. So was the cassette the reason you and your mum fell out?'

'No, the cassette was only the beginning,' I said.

By this time Betty had settled down for a tiny snoozette. Fondling her sweet, curly little ears, I told my friends about meeting Blues Hat and how he'd rocked my world with his comment about my mum making the right choice.

'Sorry, I'm confused,' Nat said, frowning. 'Can we

scroll back a bit? How did you *know* to ask your mum about the cassette?'

I felt myself flushing. 'I . . . I had a dream.' Now I'd said it aloud it sounded mad. How could something as unreal as a dream have caused my whole life to unravel?

My friends didn't seem to think it was that mad at all. In fact Ella insisted that I described everything that happened in my dream in minute detail.

When I'd finished she breathed, 'Billie, that is *SO* awesome!'

'Is it?' I said doubtfully. I just remembered how my dream had left me feeling totally haunted.

'Yes! That woman in your dream was trying to tell you something. I'm serious! My mum is totally into dreams, and she said when something like that happens in a dream it's because you're getting ready to face something, like a big family secret maybe?'

Like the fact my mum never wanted me, you mean? I thought. Did that count as a big enough secret?

'Billie, I don't know if this is important or not,' Nat said tentatively, 'but that song the mystery woman was singing on the tape, what was it?'

'It's called *Willow*,' I said. 'But I don't see—'

Nat shook her head. 'Never heard of it.'

'Nor me,' said Ella.

'Sure you have,' I said, surprised. 'Everybody knows that song.'

'Sing a bit of it,' Ella said. 'Maybe if we hear it we'll remember.'

I sang them the chorus about being someone's shelter in a storm, straight and strong like the willow.

'Oh, my God that is so beautiful,' Ella said when I'd finished. 'I've honestly never heard it before though, have you, Nat?'

Nat shook her head.

'Seriously?' For some reason I'd just assumed that everyone knew *Willow* totally off by heart the same way I knew every word, every pause and every single key change.

'A beautiful song beautifully sung,' said a voice. Mrs Nolan had been standing in the doorway. I think she hadn't wanted to interrupt my singing. 'I'm just leaving now, Natalie, but I wondered if you'd like me to make you all a nice big pot of hot chocolate before I go?'

Nat said we would like it very much.

Mrs Nolan went off to the far end of the kitchen and we heard her making busy whisking, clattering noises. She came back with a tray holding a steaming jug of frothy hot chocolate, three mugs and a small bowl of pillowy pink and white marshmallows. 'I put the marshmallows in a bowl so you can take them or leave them,' she told us. Mrs Nolan seemed way more relaxed about calories than Nat's step-mum.

After she'd gone, Ella blew out her cheeks. I could see she was still trying to take in everything I'd told them. 'I had no idea you were having such a hard time, Billie. And you never breathed one word to any of us.'

'Tell us what happened after you got back from the Grove,' said Nat. 'I know you're mad with your mum, Billie, but I can't believe she suddenly freaked out for no reason.'

I scowled at her. 'I can't help it if you don't believe it, Natalie. That's what happened.' But even as I was snapping Nat's head off, I was wondering if that was true. What had I *actually* said?

'Let's recap,' said Nat. 'You went back home and you said, "Oh, hi Mum! I've agreed to sing at a benefit to help a little girl with cerebral palsy," and *she* said, "Over my dead body, Billie Gold! Now go to your room and don't come out until you agree to my terms!"'

I had put Betty down so I could drink my hot chocolate. Now I picked her up again and let her attack my fingers with her little needle-sharp teeth. 'I might not have told her about the benefit *exactly*,' I admitted.

Ella sighed. 'You just told her you were doing a gig, didn't you?'

'No, of *course* not! Oh, I don't know,' I said miserably. 'Maybe I did. It all just seemed to blow up out of nowhere. Suddenly we were both screaming at each other. It was like, I didn't even *know* her!'

Nat and Ella were exchanging looks again. For a surreal moment I imagined they each had a hidden earpiece that was relaying the entire conversation to Lexie at the ice rink.

'OK,' said Nat briskly. 'This is what I think you should do. Go back home and have a real talk to your mum. No, don't give us that look, just listen for a moment, will you?'

'I'm with Nat,' said Ella. 'Explain to your mum about Jools holding a fundraiser. Tell her it's to raise money to send Freya to do that special programme in Arizona. Make her understand that it's not a late-night gig with prowling drug dealers, sex perverts and whatever, just local people who want to help a little kid get a life.'

I could have explained things better, I thought, swallowing. *Why didn't I?*

'I'll try,' I said huskily. 'Thanks.'

'*Then*, if she still says you can't do it, you can think about leaving home,' Ella added with a crooked little grin.

I gawped at her. Was Ella psychic? 'I never said I was leaving home! When did I say that?'

'You didn't have to,' said Ella, and she threw her arms around me and hugged me so hard it hurt and all three of us had a little cry.

I did what Nat and Ella said. I went straight home and I made myself walk into the sitting room on my jelly legs and I told Mum and Mitch that I was sorry if I hadn't explained things properly. 'But I'd like to try to tell you about it now, if that's OK,' I said, resisting the urge to run.

Mitch got up and switched off the nature programme that neither of them seemed to have been watching. 'We're listening,' he said.

They listened to my explanation without once interrupting. That was the first clue that something was up. Then Mitch turned to my mum and said quietly, 'Now that Billie's bravely broken the ice I believe it's your turn, Nina.'

Did Mitch mean it was my mum's turn to apologise to me? I saw her give him a totally desperate look, and at that moment I understood that I wasn't the only person in the room who wanted to run. That one panic-stricken look from my mum instantly undid all Nat and Ella's good work. Now I knew for sure that my mum was hiding something, something so huge that if I ever found out neither of us would ever recover.

I was suddenly so scared that my mouth had turned to cotton wool, but I didn't have a choice. I knew I couldn't live a lie. Somehow I got the words out. 'You don't need to tell me,' I said shakily. 'I've been kind of piecing it all together for a while now.'

'And what exactly do you think you've pieced together?' my mum asked scornfully, sounding like a mother in a really unconvincing movie and nothing like her normal self.

'Mum, I'm a singer and a musician. Music is who I *am*! But it's like you want to kill that part of me.'

My mum instantly stopped being in a bad movie. She looked shocked and hurt and real. 'Billie, that's not true!'

'It is *totally* true.'

She shook her head. I could see her getting agitated. 'There's things you don't know, things you didn't ever *need* to know.'

'Like the fact that you never meant to have me, you

mean?' I burst out, then after that I couldn't go on. I just stood there with my hands pressed against my mouth and whimpering like a lost little kid.

My mum's mouth opened and for a moment it was like she couldn't speak. When she found her voice, it came out sounding like she was singing and crying both at once. 'That is just *crazy*! You keep saying all these crazy things. It's like you don't trust me any more.'

'No, Mum, it's you that doesn't trust *me*!'

'Billie, of *course* I trust you.'

'You *don't*! You don't trust me to live my own life and make my own decisions, but most of all you don't trust me enough to tell me the truth.'

'When have I ever lied to you? Tell me one time!'

I felt frantic. I knew what I wanted to say but I couldn't find the words to express how crazy Mum's behaviour was making me feel. 'OK, so maybe you don't tell outright lies. You just won't tell me what's going on, like about that tape. I thought it was Dad playing his sax, so I took it, and I played it at Mr Kaminski's—'

My mum gasped. 'You heard the tape, is that what started—'

'NO!' I angrily interrupted. 'That was just like an *example*. It was just some random singer. I have no idea why you had to be so cloak and dagger about it.'

Mum was already talking over me. 'Stop, Billie, let's just stop all this, please. In all this mess, let's get one thing straight right now. I *always* wanted you. I wanted you from Day One, from the very first moment I knew.'

There was a moment's electric silence; then I just totally fell to pieces.

'Then why did he say you made the right choice?' I wailed.

'Who?' she said, bewildered.

'The man in the hat! He came to find me at Portobello Market. He asked if we had any music by Jimmie Logan.' I had huge tears rolling down my face. 'That man – he isn't – was he my dad?'

I saw my mum's expression change. *She knows who he is*, I thought.

Then she jumped to her feet. 'Of *course* he's not your dad!' she blazed. 'You were there when I got that phone call. You cried for *days*. We both did. How could you *possibly* think Jimmie was still alive?'

It was my mother's fury that convinced me. I had never seriously believed that Blues Hat was my dad. But from her reaction it was obvious that he had something major on my mum, something she didn't want me to find out.

Mitch looked totally shell-shocked. 'Billie, sweetheart, let's try to sort this out rationally instead of yelling at each other. What is it that you think you know?'

'That's just it!' I wept. 'I don't seem to know *anything* any more! I don't know if something is a memory or something I've been told or if I've totally made it all up.'

My mum covered her face with her hands.

'Nina you've got to tell her.' Mitch sounded drained. 'Tell her tonight, before this entire family goes insane.'

I have never seen my mum look so scared. 'I can't! I promised myself I'd never—'

'For Pete's sake, *I'll* tell her then,' my step-dad said, exasperated. 'Then at least it'll be out in the open once and for all.'

I closed my eyes. I didn't know if I'd ever be ready for this.

When Mitch eventually spoke, his voice was gentle again. 'The singer on the tape, Billie, did you really not recognise her voice?'

I opened my eyes again in surprise because I could tell he was smiling and I didn't think there was that much to smile about.

Mitch reached out and clasped my mum's hand in his. 'Billie, let me introduce you to a brilliantly talented but little-known singer called Nina Gold.'

Chapter Twelve

That was it. That was the dark secret that was blowing my family apart. In movies, after the big revelation, everyone is laughing and joking, the soundtrack swells, the credits roll and everyone walks out of the cinema feeling great.

We were just really subdued. We made hot drinks, carefully washed and dried our mugs. We were quiet and shocked, like people who had just survived a car crash.

It was close to midnight when we finally separated to go to bed. Mitch went into the bathroom to brush his teeth. Mum and I lingered outside my bedroom door. I had all kinds of questions buzzing round my head, about Blues Hat, about why my mum stopped singing, about my dad, but I just said softly, 'When Finlay was poorly, were you singing *Willow*?'

Mum nodded. Her eyes were red from crying.

'The song was in my dream that night,' I said slowly. 'Did you ever sing that song to me, when I was little?'

Again she nodded. 'For some reason that was the only song that helped you get back to sleep when you'd had bad dreams.' Mum took a breath. 'I've been thinking, and I just wanted to say one more thing. You said you promised Jools you'd sing at Freya's benefit. I'm still not happy about it, but I suppose your school work wouldn't suffer if it's just this once.'

I could feel how scary it was for her to make this concession, but I felt like crying. I so badly wanted my mum to *want* to be there, but no way was I going to beg.

There was a brief highly-charged silence, then I said stiffly, 'Thanks. Night, Mum.'

My mum looked sad but firm. 'Night, Billie.'

It was all too much to take in. I needed to sleep. I needed not to have to think, yet as I tossed and turned in the dark, complicated new thoughts kept pushing to the front of my mind. All this time I'd assumed I'd got my music genes from my dad. Now it seemed I'd got them from both sides. My mum the social worker had turned out to be my mum the former singer. She wasn't the same person any more.

Which meant that I wasn't either.

Next day at school Nat and Ella came rushing up, wanting to know how things had gone.

'Do you mind if we save it for Saturday?' I asked. 'I'm not being weird, honestly, but I've got to do this benefit on almost no sleep. At the moment it feels like I need to focus on that, just to get through it.'

'You're OK though, yeah?' said Nat.

'I'm OK,' I promised.

'And you aren't going to leave home and beg outside the tube and have a cute dog on a long piece of string?' Ella said, trying to make a joke out of it.

I shook my head. 'If I do decide to get a dog on a string though, I will steal Ugly Betty. I bet people would give me loads of money if I had Betty.'

'Would it be OK if we came to see you at the Grove?' asked Ella. 'I mean, tell us if it will put you off, Billie, but it would be so cool to come and see our friend performing at her first gig.'

I was so touched. 'Really? You really want to be there?'

'Of course we want to be there! So does Lexie.'

All my friends wanted to come to support me. But

not my mum – the one person who should understand how important tonight was to me. That really hurt. I wanted Mum to be proud of me. I wanted her to stand up at the end of my set and say, 'That's my daughter up on stage. Isn't she amazing?'

At least she had agreed to let me perform, I thought. What was that jokey card Mr Kaminski had propped up on his mantelpiece?

The impossible we can do immediately. Miracles take a little longer.

The benefit started at 7.30. This meant all the artists had to be at the Grove an hour before the event kicked off. Jools was there, flying around in the most amazing tight-fitting black dress and sparkly earrings, thanking us for coming and telling us we were all going to be brilliant. She introduced everyone to Ann-Marie, Freya's mum.

'You look gorgeous,' she told me.

'You look gorgeous yourself,' I told her truthfully. 'You are absolutely glowing.'

'Actually, I'll soon be having some exciting news to share with you,' she said. 'It's still under wraps at the moment, but I'll be telling everyone just as soon as we've got the benefit out of the way. You're not too

214

nervous, are you?' she asked, patting my shoulder.

'I'm terrified,' I confessed. 'But I absolutely can't wait!'

My set was scheduled for the middle of the evening. I was sandwiched between a stand-up comedian and a local hip hop group formed entirely of streetwise little ten- and eleven-year-olds.

Jools was the MC for the whole show. I waited in the wings with my heart pounding as she told the audience that they were really privileged because they were going to be the first people in London to hear the fabulous Billie Gold, who was only fourteen but was going to be huge very soon.

As I ran on with my guitar, I had the weirdest feeling of déjà vu. I remembered my dream of the club with the mystery woman in the sparkling evening dress; the mystery woman who had turned out to be my own mother.

Then suddenly there I was, dazzled by the spotlights, looking out at all the people. The club was rammed full. I hadn't expected that.

Wow! I thought. This wasn't a dream. This was actually happening for real! And in that moment everything else just melted away and I gave a little bounce of pure joy and waved merrily at the audience.

'Hello and thanks for coming, everyone!' I greeted

them. 'I'm going to sing you a song I wrote called *Notting Hill Girls*. I'm singing it because I'm proud of where I live and all my Notting Hill friends. It's also a tribute to a really special little Notting Hill girl who is close to all our hearts tonight. I'm expecting all of you to dig deep into your pockets so we can send Freya to Arizona to get the treatment she needs, and then she'll be able to strut around with all the rest of us bold, beautiful, feisty girls from Notting Hill!'

People cheered and clapped. I saw Freya's mum say something to her friend and wipe her eyes.

Jools and I had agreed that I should sing *Notting Hill Girls* first because it would get everyone into a positive party mood. As my backing track came on I took a huge breath and launched into my song. If I say so myself, it is a kicking little tune and the lyrics always make me smile. There's a feel-good chorus about swinging along through Portobello with the wind in our hair and the world at our feet. By the time I'd finished the whole club was buzzing.

My second song was a comedy number I wrote about a girl who changes her styles and her opinions every time she dates a different boy. It's called *True Colours* like the old Cindi Lauper song and it starts with the same chords, but then it turns into a little hip hop thing only with the *True Colours* chorus coming in and out.

I felt relaxed enough to look around at the audience now. I eventually spotted my friends and some other kids from our school; also Dino and his crew, plus one of his girlfriends. Then to my utter amazement I spotted Mr Berolli! For a moment I thought I might actually faint. Then I saw him smiling and nodding to the beat, looking like he was totally enjoying himself, so I just gave him a cheeky little wave and carried on singing.

After *True Colours*, I quickly retuned my guitar.

'I didn't write this song,' I said. 'I wish I had, but a brilliant singer-songwriter called Joan Armatrading got there first. It's called *Willow* and my mother recently told me she used to sing it like a lullaby when I was a baby and I couldn't sleep.' And I played the soft slow opening chords and began to sing.

Willow is one of those magical songs where people get so totally taken over by the music that they just can't help themselves; they naturally start swaying and joining in with the chorus. People started to hold up their mobiles, snapping pictures of me up on stage. I could see the lights from the camera phones like fireflies flashing on and off. Suddenly there was an especially bright flash and I saw my mum in the aisle taking my picture.

Miracles take a little longer.

I thought my heart was going to burst. She'd come. My mum had actually come! As I sang the last oh-so-soft-and-slow chorus about the sun coming up, I could see her silently shaping the words.

When I finished there was pure dead silence for a couple of heartbeats. Then everybody went crazy, clapping and stomping and calling my name.

Somewhere in the mayhem I heard my mum telling someone, 'That's my daughter! Billie Gold is my daughter!'

Chapter Thirteen

That night I ended up staying out 'til really late, like a real bona fide rock chick. But my mum couldn't exactly tell me off. It was her I was staying out with!

After we'd left the Grove, she took me to a little hole-in-the-wall restaurant called My Big Fat Greek Cupboard that she and Mitch sometimes go to. I'd been too nervous to eat before the show so I was absolutely starving. Our conversation over dinner got quite intense at times, but it was me, not my mum, who finally realised we were the only diners left in the *taverna*.

'Oh my God, is that the time!' I squeaked, looking at my watch.

'Relax, it's the weekend,' said my mum. 'We can all have a lie-in.'

'You have a lie-in if you want, old lady,' I teased. 'I've got to be in Portobello at ten-thirty sharp!'

Despite my late night, I was up, showered, dressed and out of the house by 9.55 a.m. I whisked Bullet around the block so fast his stumpy little legs hardly touched the ground.

When I got back with a breathless Bullet, Mr Kaminski said eagerly, 'How did your concert go, Billie? Did they raise the money for that little girl?'

'It went great,' I told him. 'I don't think they know how much money they raised yet. Sorry, Mr Kaminski, I've got to run. I'll be back to walk Bullet later, yeah?'

I was singing to myself as I hurried to catch the bus. Since everything else in my life was working out so well, I was absolutely sure that today was the day the Breakfast Club was finally going to track down the perfect café!

We'd decided to start today's quest with Café Blush. It's just a few doors down from where Hugh Grant had his imaginary travel bookshop in the *Notting Hill* movie. It's such a cool location that I was secretly hoping this was The One.

I arrived to see my friends already waiting outside. As soon as they caught sight of me turning into the street, they all rushed at me and started hugging and congratulating me right there in the middle of the pavement, making people stop and stare.

I don't know why they didn't use Café Blush in that *Notting Hill* movie. It's in one of those narrow old Portobello houses that are painted all funky colours. Café Blush wasn't painted pink as I'd imagined, but a deep hyacinth blue. It was just the sign that was pink, a hot glowing pink like flamingo feathers.

The minute we stepped inside I felt a nice mellow little buzz. They were playing an old hip hop track by the Black Eyed Peas. It easily felt like the kind of place where you might spot an off-duty celeb blowing the froth off her cappuccino.

'Music and ambience five stars,' I said, beaming.

'I'm totally loving the decor,' said Ella approvingly.

The café's colour scheme somehow managed to be cool but also fun; mainly pale grey and duck-egg blue with little touches of flamingo pink and primrose yellow. The tables were covered in spotty red and white oilcloth that made the café cheerful and homely at the same time. The posters on the walls had upbeat messages in beautiful graphics like *Wake up and Smell the Roses* and *The Magic Starts Here*.

Ella gave me a nudge. '"The Magic Starts Here!"'

she said in a stage whisper. 'This is so totally Breakfast Club!'

The café was already really busy. Luckily, unlike at the Hub, they had plenty of waiters and waitresses efficiently whizzing about balancing huge numbers of plates of absolutely mouth-watering food. They all looked crisply unisex in natty black waistcoats over white shirts and blue jeans. A waiter came up to us straightaway and showed us to a table. He was perfectly polite and friendly, but I did notice that he seemed just the littlest bit surprised.

For obvious reasons, we were all a bit over-excited that morning. Plus, when we saw the incredibly delicious food other customers were eating, we got even more excited! Without bothering to check the prices we cheerfully ordered fruit salads with yoghurt and home-made granola, a selection of croissants (almond, chocolate, apricot and plain) and cappuccinos that were so fabulously fluffy they came with their own chocolate-sprinkled little clouds!

We all agreed that the fruit salads were perfect, not too sweet and not too sour. They hadn't cheated by bulking it out with flavourless lumps of apple like those disappointing fruit salads you get in supermarkets. The yoghurt was so creamy it was more like actual cream.

But the croissants were totally out of this world!

Ella's first astonished mouthful reduced her to utter silence. Then she said rapturously, 'Oh. My. God. I bet these are the same croissants they give angels for breakfast!'

'These are so good I want to cry!' Nat literally sounded as if she might be on the verge of bursting into tears. Then she added wistfully, 'They're very nearly as divine as those *dolce* that Jools gave us the first time we went to Mario's.'

'Yeah, well, nothing's ever going to top those,' Lexie said.

I shook my head. 'No, never.'

And without meaning to I let out a regretful little sigh. There was a moment's silence as we all remembered how completely perfect Mario's had been.

Then Nat gave herself a little shake. 'But hey, this is definitely the best cafe we've been to since Mario's.'

'Definitely,' we all agreed.

When we had made a big dent in the plate of pastries, Ella briskly dusted the croissant crumbs off her hands and said, 'Right! It's time for Billie to spill!'

'Yeah, Billie!' said Nat. 'When you and your mum went off together last night you both looked so happy. What happened?'

'Don't worry, Billie,' Lexie interrupted with a grin. 'I made Ella and Nat get me up to speed before you showed up. They gave me the whole back-story: the dream cassette that turned out to be real, your mum freaking about you being a singer, the mysterious guy with the hat . . .'

I did a nervous laugh. 'Wow, lucky my bus was late, huh?'

I set down my half-empty mug and my three friends unconsciously hitched their chairs closer to our table. 'I don't really know where to start,' I admitted. 'So much has happened since I came back to your house, Nat.'

'Start with the most major thing,' advised Nat, 'and go on from there.'

I blew out my breath. 'The most major thing is I found out my mum had a secret, and it . . . well, the fact is, it changes everything.'

'How come nothing dramatic like that happens to me?' Lexie complained at once. 'Nobody in my family ever has any secrets!'

'Lexie!' Ella hissed. 'Billie's *talking*?'

'Sorry, Billie, didn't mean to ruin your big moment,' Lexie said apologetically.

I hesitated. I was still getting my head around this

myself. 'My mum used to be a singer,' I said in a rush.

Nat gasped. 'You are kidding!'

Ella looked puzzled. '*That's* her dark secret? Why did it have to be a secret?'

Lexie nodded. 'You could understand if she'd been, like, working for MI6, but a singer is such a cool thing to be. Why wouldn't she want you to know?'

I'd asked my mum this exact question in the taverna last night. I started fiddling with my hair, trying to find the right words. 'How my mum explained it to me, it wasn't like she'd been living a double life; more like her life had just naturally split into two separate lives.'

Lexie pulled a face. 'Sorry, Billie, you've lost me already.'

I tried to explain it better. 'Before she had me, all she could think about was how to get known as a singer. She lived and breathed and dreamed music. She hung about with other singers and musicians—'

'That sounds like you,' Nat interrupted.

'Is that how she met your dad?' Lexie asked.

I nodded. It seemed weird now that I had never asked her how they'd met. Or maybe I had and she'd just steered me away.

'Was your mum really famous?' Ella asked eagerly. 'Did she have a recording contract or something?'

225

'No, she wasn't ever famous. She and dad were both starting to get known when my mum found out she was pregnant with me.'

I told my friends that even though they were poor as mice, both my parents had been really excited about having a baby on the way. They were both innocently convinced that having a baby wouldn't stop them pursuing their careers.

My mum had said her first inkling that combining music and babies might not be so easy was when she and Dad went to a party. Some of the people in their crowd already had little kids that they towed around with them everywhere. When Mum went to the bedroom at the end of the night to get her coat, she couldn't find it anywhere. Then she heard whimpering and discovered someone's little toddler curled up fast asleep on it in the dark. The little kid was still quietly sobbing in its sleep. No one had heard it crying through the noise of the party.

Mum said at first she was able to take me along to gigs in my carry cot and I'd sleep through the whole thing. But once I started to toddle it was more of a problem. She couldn't exactly just stick me in a corner with a rusk, and she and Dad were still too poor to pay a sitter.

Dad was having his own worries. My mum said he was a brilliant musician but it was almost like he'd been born at the wrong time. His kind of music, the music he loved, wasn't the kind kids were dancing to in the nineties. Dad had always had a dream of working in a jazz club in New York. He told my mum they should leave this country and make a fresh start in the US. He'd got a friend who could get them work in a club. They'd both make their names and live happily ever after.

But my mum didn't believe that the grass was going to be any greener in New York. For one thing she wouldn't know a soul, except for my dad. She was also concerned about how she'd take care of me. She kept thinking of that little kid crying itself to sleep on a pile of coats.

'I loved Jimmie and I loved music,' she told me. Then her memories suddenly got too painful for her to go on eating and she had to set down her knife and fork and take a few breaths before she went on. 'But I couldn't stand to think of you being dragged around to parties and clubs. I'd seen how some musicians lived, hand to mouth, their families always coming way down the list.'

Then my mum found out that my dad owed some

dodgy people a lot of money. She realised this could be one of the reasons he was so keen to leave London. Mum confronted him with it right away, telling him nothing could be solved by running away. She said it would be better to stay in London and face up to their problems; they could sort them out together. My dad agreed. He said running away when things didn't work out seemed to have become a bad habit, but he had a beautiful little daughter to take care of now and he wanted to change.

My friends' eyes never left my face as I described what happened next.

'A few nights after they'd had this conversation, while my mum was giving me my bath, my dad packed his bags and left.' I had to stop and blink back my tears. I still vividly remembered that terrible night.

'I came out of the bathroom giggling with Mum. She'd washed my hair and it was all wrapped up in a towel. She was calling out to my dad about something I'd done that she thought was really cute, then she realised he wasn't answering. She went rushing into their bedroom. I went rushing after her, not understanding what was wrong, and all the drawers were standing open like we'd been burgled. We never saw him again.'

My friends all knew that my dad had left us, but I

think this was the first time they understood just how hard it had been on me and Mum.

After a long silence, Nat said, 'Did your mum ever tell you how your dad died?'

'His friend found him dead in his chair in the early hours of the morning,' I said shakily. 'My mum said he had a weak heart.'

'Oh my God, the poor man,' breathed Ella. 'Dying all alone in a strange country.'

I nodded tearfully. 'I know.'

Lexie's mouth had set in a disapproving little line. 'Well, I'm sorry, but I can't believe he just walked out and left you and your mum without even leaving a note.'

I shook my head. 'My mum said she truly believes that in his mind my dad never intended to leave us forever. He wrote a letter before he flew out of Gatwick, telling her he expected to be back in a year or two. He said he'd be coming back as a success. He'd have made a big pile of money and be able to buy us a nice house and all the other things my mum and I deserved.'

'But that didn't happen,' said Nat softly.

'No, it didn't happen. My mum cried herself to sleep for about a week. Then she says one morning she woke up and thought, right: it's up to me now. She decided that her old life as a singer was over, and she went and found herself a job, signed up for some night classes, and eventually she trained as a social worker.'

'So that's what Blues Hat meant when he said your mum made the right choice,' said Ella.

I could feel a stray tear crawling down my cheek and quickly swiped it away. 'His real name is Lloyd but Mum said everyone mostly just called him Lips. He's a brilliant clarinet player apparently and was a close friend of Dad's. When my mum told him that she was giving up her singing career, he gave her a really hard time, telling her she was betraying Dad's memory by selling out. She had a gift and gifts are supposed to be used, blah blah. My mum told him she loved singing but she loved her daughter more.'

The exact words my mum had used to Lloyd were, 'I love singing, Lloyd, but I love my daughter more than anything on this Earth.' When she told me that, I cried into my ice-cream.

Your mother made the right choice.

How different those words sounded now that I knew which choice my mum had made, and that for her it was no choice at all.

Mum hadn't seen Lloyd the Lips for years, then the other day she'd bumped into him outside Kids'

Company and they'd gone into Starbucks for a quick catch-up. Lloyd said he'd always wondered how we were and how Jimmie's little girl had grown up, and on impulse Mum told him that if he went to Portobello that afternoon he'd be able to see me at Vaughan's Vinyl stall.

My mum said she'd regretted it the minute he'd gone. 'I should have known he'd pull some silly stunt.' Mum had successfully kept her two lives separate for so long that her old life had begun to feel like a dream, like it never actually happened. Now all her old ghosts were suddenly whooshing out of the closet. Me confronting her about the cassette, unexpectedly running into Lloyd, stirring up things she'd hoped to keep locked away forever.

I noticed Ella surreptitiously dabbing up the few remaining croissant crumbs. She popped them into her mouth and quickly licked her lips. 'OK, Billie, I kind of understand why your mum felt she had to give up singing. I just don't get why she felt she had to totally hide it from you all this time?'

'I do,' Nat piped up. 'Because she didn't want Billie to think she'd made this huge sacrifice.'

I nodded. 'That was totally it, Nat. She said she couldn't lay that kind of burden on me. She couldn't bear for me to grow up thinking she'd given up her big dream just to be my mum.'

My mum had reached across our dessert plates and caught hold of my hand. 'I want you to know that I never regretted my decision. I've never once wished I could have any part of that old life back. You were the real deal for me, Billie, is that clear?' Then we had both smelled singeing fabric and I'd hastily moved our little red tea-light before my mum's sleeve totally caught fire.

'My mum said she had loved singing so much, but she realised now that she was never temperamentally cut out for that life,' I told my friends.

Then she'd said something I'd never imagined I would hear her say. 'Talent is only one part of being a singer, Billie. You have to have real guts or you'll never be able to deal with all the hard knocks. What I saw tonight showed me that you not only have talent, you're an incredibly strong person. I think you could go the extra distance, if it's what you really want.'

I had stared at her and my eyes had slowly filled with tears. 'But won't you mind?'

'This is your life, Billie, your one and only life,' she'd told me and I saw tears shining in her eyes too. 'I've made my choices. Now it's your turn.'

We'd hugged slightly awkwardly across the table and I'd felt a huge weight lifting off me, a weight I'd been carrying my whole life without even knowing.

'Did your mum really never ever sing again?' Ella asked. 'If I had a real gift like her, I don't think I could just, like, *totally* cut it out of my life.'

'Nor me,' I admitted. When I'd asked my mum that question she'd given me a surprisingly mischievous smile. 'I sing in the car sometimes with the windows rolled up. Extremely therapeutic when you've spent the day with a bunch of stroppy kids!'

Nat gave a little shiver as if someone had walked over her grave. 'It's so weird to think that you and your mum might have never sorted this out, Billie, if you hadn't dreamed that dream. Actually, it's kind of spooky. I never heard of anyone dreaming a true dream before.'

'I've already *explained* about that,' Ella said impatiently.

'You never explained it to me,' Lexie told her. 'I just got the back-story, remember?'

For Lexie's benefit, Ella repeated her mum's theory that dreams sometimes come when it's finally time for people to bring things out into the open. 'Your mum probably couldn't have coped with it before, but she can now because she's finally over what happened with your dad, plus she's all settled and happy with Mitch.'

I nodded. 'I think you're right.' For the first few years after Finlay was born you could always feel my mum secretly waiting for Mitch to run off and leave us like my dad.

'Maybe, deep down, your mum didn't want to keep her secret from you, Billie,' suggested Nat solemnly.

Lexie was getting fidgety. 'No offence, Billie,' she said, patting my hand, 'but this is getting *way* too deep for me. I vote we order some more of those super-fluffy cappuccinos and at least one more heavenly croissant each!'

I felt a sudden twang of worry as I remembered that we had never actually looked at the prices. 'Can we afford it though?'

'My treat,' said Ella at once. 'My dad sent me some money. You're a local celeb now, Billie, you deserve a bit of luxury!'

'Aw, thanks, Ella,' I said gratefully. 'I still think we should check the menus though.'

Of course, the waiter had taken our menus away after we'd ordered. Using the pretence of going to the loo, Lexie stealthily removed a menu from a big stack by the cash desk. When she got back to our table, she opened it and quickly shut it again. 'Oh my God.'

She passed the menu around, and one by one we snapped it shut and turned pale. Now we understood the waiter's surprise. Café Blush was *seriously* pricey. Basically, we could have bought a small Caribbean island just for what we'd spent so far.

'Zero stars for prices,' Ella said forlornly. 'No, make that minus zero.'

'I really thought this was going to be The One,' said Nat.

'No more café hunting for us this weekend, that's for sure,' Lexie said.

'What are we going to do if we can't pay?' I had visions of police cars racing through Portobello, coming to take us to jail.

We did some frantic adding up. Even with Ella's money from her dad, we were about four quid short. Normally I'd have my pay from Ozzie's, but I'd had to cancel because of Freya's fundraiser.

We were just emptying out our purses and anxiously counting out those fiddly five-pence pieces that always get stuck in the corners, when who should come into the cafe but Mr Berolli!

He was wearing his long charity-shop coat with the dangling threads and a lovely fawn and duck-egg blue scarf that looked really good with his colouring. He was with an older male friend. He spotted us and immediately came over, giving us no chance to hide our pathetic little piles of coins.

'I didn't expect to see you lot here,' he said.

'And you won't be seeing us here again,' Lexie said under her breath.

I deliberately trod on her foot. 'Shut up!' I hissed.

'I just wanted to tell you how much I enjoyed your performance last night, Billie,' Josh Berolli told me. 'Jools had mentioned you were a singer but I had no idea you were going to be so amazing, well done!'

'I didn't know you knew Jools,' I said in surprise.

'I've known her my whole life! She's my second cousin – no, hang on . . .' He silently counted up on his fingers. 'Maybe she's my third cousin. Some kind of cousin by marriage anyway.' He gave us one of his totally heart-stopping grins. 'Anyway, whichever kind of cousins we are, I'm sure you'll be glad to know they raised a lot of money last night.'

'Fantastic,' I said. 'Did they actually reach the total?'

'Jools said all the money isn't in yet. The benefit was just one of loads of fundraising events people have been organising around Notting Hill. But I think she said they're only something like a couple of thousand pounds off their target now.' He gave us another beam. 'I'd say it's looking fairly definite that Freya and her mum will be going to Arizona!'

'That's fantastic,' I said again.

There was an awkward moment while we all fidgeted, not wanting to be rude but inwardly panicking about how we were going to pay our humungous bill. To our surprise Mr Berolli leaned closer to our table and dropped his voice to a stage whisper. 'So what's the food like here? It was Mark's idea to come. I've never been before.'

'Nor have we, sir!' Ella couldn't resist flashing him a flirty little smile. 'We just came here because we're auditioning cafés.'

'Is that what you're up to?' he said, amused. 'I don't think I've heard of anyone holding auditions for cafés before.'

'We used to go out for breakfast at Mario's on Saturdays,' I explained. 'Now that it's closed we're, like, hunting for a new venue.'

'Oh, right!' Mr Berolli suddenly looked tickled about something. 'I might have an update for you there.' He suddenly remembered his friend. 'Do you mind grabbing a table, Mark, and ordering us a couple of lattes?' he asked in an apologetic tone. 'I'll be with you in a sec.'

Then Josh Berolli gave us some totally mind-boggling news.

Mario had had an elderly widowed aunt who had been living with them for years. A few weeks ago she had been taken to hospital and had just recently died. Mario's aunt was once married to an incredibly wealthy man but they had never had children, so she had left all her money to Mario and his family! Mr Berolli didn't know exactly how much. He said Jools mentioned so many zeros that his brain went completely numb. Since the sale of his old café had fallen through, Mario had been able to buy the whole premises outright!

We stared at Josh Berolli, open-mouthed. Then we jumped to our feet squealing and hugging each other in a most immature manner while everyone, including Mr Berolli's friend, gave us sympathetic if baffled smiles.

'You know what this means?' Ella said in a breathless gap between hugs. 'We can stop the auditions! Now we've got Mario's back we can have breakfast there every Saturday forever!'

'Whyever didn't Jools tell me last night?' I wondered.

Then I remembered that she had mentioned some good news that she wasn't allowed to share quite yet. I'd just been too caught up in my first proper gig to take it in.

'I wish she had!' Lexie said ruefully. 'We could have saved ourselves a fortune!'

'This café is really expensive,' Ella whispered to Mr Berolli. 'I mean, like, *horrendously* expensive.'

'I did notice you'd been emptying out your pockets.' I noticed that Mr Berolli was tactfully keeping his voice down. 'I can lend you a fiver if that would help?'

I could feel myself getting hot with embarrassment. 'We're just two pounds fifty short, sir. If you could just loan us that, I promise you can have it back first thing Monday morning.'

'No problem,' he said grinning, and cheerfully handed over a fiver. 'It's not like you to be so quiet, Natalie,' he teased her.

All this time Nat had seemed totally tongue-tied. It was clear that she was dying to ask Josh Berolli something, but madly fighting down the urge because she was so determined to be a reformed character. But as soon as our teacher spoke to her, she totally couldn't hold back any longer. 'So where's Miss Simpson today, sir?' she blurted.

Mr Berolli looked surprised. 'I don't know, Natalie,'

he said, 'but I'd imagine she's probably with her fiancé.'

Poor Nat! She went SO red. 'I never knew Miss Simpson had a fiancé,' she stuttered.

'Strange as it might seem, teachers do actually have private lives,' he told her coolly. 'Anyway, good to see you all, and really well done, Billie.'

He went off to join his friend, leaving us reeling.

'Oh my God,' Nat whispered. 'How totally stupid do I feel?'

'If it helps, I'm feeling pretty stupid too,' Ella whispered back.

'I don't feel stupid, just confused,' said Lexie. 'I thought you said he and Miss Simpson were like, an *item*?'

'Lexie, can you please keep your voice down?' Nat begged.

Unfortunately our collective embarrassment wasn't over yet. We had to count out all our little piles of change for the friendly waiter and then he had to carefully count them all over again to check we'd added up right. We were like those old ladies you get stuck behind in supermarkets who don't have enough for a sad little tin of ravioli.

As soon as we got outside we had to vent our feelings

in another squeal and hug fest.

'I can't *believe* it!' Ella said. 'We were literally *rescued* by Josh Berolli! How incredibly cool was that?'

'And he's still single!' I reminded them.

'Oh my God, you're right!!' Ella squealed. 'And next Saturday we'll be back in our favourite booth at Mario's with Lily Allen and Dizzee Rascal smiling down on us!'

'We might not be back in our booth by next Saturday,' I pointed out. 'It's going to take a couple of weeks or so to sort out.'

'OK, not next week but really soon,' said Ella. 'Oh my God, I have SO missed Mario's coffee!'

'And those little booths where you can be private,' said Lexie. 'And I missed Jools. She's such a laugh.'

'And the *dolce*!' Nat's furious blushes were finally fading. 'I am seriously going to cry now.'

'And the music,' I reminded them. 'Mario's had the best music.'

Without meaning to, we were all stealing wistful glances through the window of the café. We could see Mr Berolli chatting to his friend while they waited for their terrifyingly expensive food.

'Do you think he's telling his friend Mark about us?' Nat asked hopefully. From the possessive way she said

'Mark', I knew she had mentally logged the name to add to her Mr Berolli file.

Ella gave a lovelorn sigh. 'I can't believe he lent us the money to pay our bill. He has to be the loveliest teacher anyone ever had. Remember how amazing he was to you, Billie, when he caught you tearing up that picture of Shrek – I mean, Miss Simpson?'

Lexie did her mischievous little grin. 'Poor Nat! You went to all that trouble to get your revenge and it turns out they aren't even going out?'

I hadn't told Lexie about Nat's Photoshop stunt. Ella must have filled her in.

'Can we not talk about that, Lexie?' Nat begged. She'd gone fiery red again.

'Ooh, Nat, what happened? I thought you were one of the bad girls now,' Lexie teased.

I could see that Lexie was dying to get more mileage out of the Shrek story, but Nat totally didn't need that so I quickly made a joke out of it. 'Natalie just went over to the Dark Side for a while, but now she's back, aren't you?'

Lexie shook her head pityingly. 'You do know you three are all totally bonkers? All I can say is you're lucky there's at least one sane person in the Breakfast Club.'

'And that's you, is it?' I asked, raising my eyebrows,

and all four of us went off into fits of giggles.

Still giggling, we linked arms and went swinging down the street. I kept seeing our four laughing faces reflecting back from shop windows. We looked so good! We looked like the girls in my song; the girls with the wind in their hair and the world at their feet. We were the Breakfast Club!

Read the second story...

Friendship, Fun and a table for Four...

Meet

Natalie's size zero stepsister Plum is getting married and Natalie's going to be a bridesmaid. She's dreading it. Her stepmum and her other sister Nelly are super-skinny too and Natalie knows they think she's the odd one out.

Billie, Ella and Lexie are adamant that Nat should stay exactly as she is and not give into the pressure, but as the wedding looms, Nat's self-esteem is shrinking and so is her personality. Can the Breakfast Club help her get back on track?

Kate Costelloe

Nat's Bridesmaid Blues

hodderchildrens.co.uk

Gallagher Academy
might claim to be a school
for geniuses – but it's really
a school for spies.

Cammie Morgan is fluent in fourteen languages
and capable of killing a man in seven different ways
(three of which involve a piece of uncooked spaghetti).

But she's only just beginning her most dangerous
mission yet – falling in love…

Don't miss all four books in Ally Carter's
Gallagher Girls series

78 1 40830 951 3 £5.99 PB
78 1 40831 412 8 £5.99 eBook

978 1 40830 952 0 £5.99 PB
978 1 40831 414 2 £5.99 eBook

978 1 40830 953 7 £5.99 PB
978 1 40831 439 5 £5.99 eBook

978 1 40830 954 4 £5.99 PB
978 1 40831 541 5 £5.99 eBook

www.gallagheracademy.co.uk
www.facebook.com/gallagheracademy
ORCHARD BOOKS

Don't forget to visit
www.gallagheracademy.co.uk -
home of Ally Carter's
Gallagher Girls!

Find out all about the Gallagher Girls books
and author Ally Carter, listen to
Cammie Morgan podcasts, watch trailers,
enter exclusive competitions and sign up to
the Gallagher Girls newsletter.

Win!

Visit now to enter the competition
to be one of the first people in the UK
to get their hands on a copy of
Ally Carter's new book,
Heist Society.

Terms and Conditions apply,
visit www.gallagheracademy.co.uk
for all the details

978 1 40830 955 1 £5.99 PB SEPT 2011
978 1 40831 567 5 £5.99 eBook SEPT 2011

www.gallagheracademy.co.uk
www.facebook.com/gallagheracademy

ORCHARD BOOKS

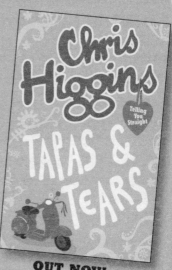

Chris Higgins

Telling You Straight

"KEPT ME HOOKED"
Chicklish

Eva wants to be the best at everything, just like her older sister, Amber. She's queen of the gym club and the girl everyone envies.

But when new girl Patty arrives in town, cracks begin to show in her perfect life and it's time for Eva to confront some hidden secrets ...

OUT NOW